When Libby Lost Her Smile

by

Naomi Parker

STRATEGIC BOOK GROUP

Strategic Book Group
P.O. Box 333
Durham CT 06422
www.StrategicBookClub.com

ISBN: 978-1-60976-037-3

Printed in the United States of America

Book Design: Bonita S. Watson

Contents

FIGHT THE FIGHT

I'm a nobody. I am not famous. I don't have a college degree. I'm not rich. I've never been on TV; I'm just a nobody like so many people around us every day. I could be you, your next door neighbor, your sister, or that pain in the butt mother who keeps showing up at the school where you work.

I am however fighting a fight I never in my years would have dreamed I'd be fighting. I am fighting red tape, school policies, attorneys, insurance companies, and overall, a general misunderstanding of what it means to be the mother of a child with a disability.

I've learned that the word classified doesn't necessarily mean an ad in the paper, and I've had so many initials thrown at me, my head swims with visions of CSE, FAPE, IEP, IDEA, TBI, PTSD, NOS, and on and on, and I've learned that I am not alone.

There are mothers and fathers out there fighting the same fight, feeling the same frustrations, not knowing what the next step is. I've met them and gotten to know some of them personally. Every story is different, yet the same. Every disability is unique to the person living with that disability and their families, but when push comes to shove it's the same fight.

This is our story, a story that starts Sept. 25, 2006, when our fourteen-year-old daughter, Elizabeth, was in a school-bus accident that left her with mild traumatic brain injury. It's the story of how lives can change in an instant and the struggle to find our "normal." Along the journey for those reading this, my hope is that you find strength in your own journey, because it's a battle that we, as parents, wake up to every morning wondering what this new day will bring. It's the story of a hidden disability that due to organizations like the Brain Injury Association, and the Bob Woodruff Foundation (Remind.org) is finally getting some of the recognition it deserves.

But, like I said, I'm not a celebrity, or a doctor and this really isn't a how-to book. It's the story of a family in a small rural community fighting for their daughter's rights while trying to get on with life around them, learning to find that happy medium between driving ourselves crazy with what happened yesterday and calmly trying to prepare for tomorrow and dealing with right now, all at the same time.

The names in this story are fictional with the exception of the three organizations that helped us and the people that supported us. I want to protect my daughter's future. She doesn't want to be known as that girl with the brain injury her entire life and I respect that. The names of the school and town aren't important. What is important is that it could be your school or your town. What happens in this book comes straight from the journal that I kept through our journey.

CHAPTER I

It's just a concussion

I never thought I'd get tired of hearing this one innocent little phrase, "It's just a concussion." Maybe it was the "just a" part that bothered me, or possibly it's because the word "concussion" itself is such a broad term. It can cover anything from getting a slight bump on the head that leaves a person with a headache for a couple days, to almost total memory loss, confusion, mind boggling pressure headaches and cognitive impairments that can last for years. It was something I never really thought that much about except on the odd occasion when someone I knew was in an accident and I was told "It's just a concussion" almost making light of the fact they'd been in an accident.

My husband Dave and I raised two very active boys who played football and rode bikes without helmets. Back then, like seatbelts, it wasn't something most people thought about. I didn't mind the seat belt laws or the bike helmet laws. Once they were in effect I followed them, and to me the laws made sense, but gosh, when I was a kid, or our boys were kids, we just hopped in the car or on a bike without any thought of protection.

1

A couple months before Dave and I were married, he took a fall at work, landing on his head, on a concrete pad, eight feet below. Dave broke his knee in the fall, and sustained a concussion. We joked about his hard head and in all honesty, didn't think much about it because he didn't seem to have any adverse effects, other than a mild headache. He wore a cast from toe to hip for six weeks and walked with a cane for another month after that, and that was that.

It actually became a reality again when our oldest boy Peyton got a concussion during a high school football game. Two players from the opposing side double teamed him, hitting him so hard his helmet flew off. As a sport's mom, it was my worst nightmare watching my son go limp, holding my breath waiting to see movement, forcing myself to stay rooted to my seat and not run foolishly out on the field. I wait as the coaches run out and kneel over my still motionless baby boy and then yes, there it is, movement, as slight as it is, it allows me to let out the breath I'd been holding. I relax a little as he walks unassisted beside the coaches to the sidelines.

"Wait, what's Peyton doing rolling around on the ground? That's not right," I think to myself. The coaches call me down from my seat on the bleachers to see what I think because they too see the change. My always cool, popular, wouldn't be caught dead doing something that would draw anything but admiration in his direction, son, was crawling around on the ground, spitting streams of water into the air on the sidelines.

My fears were again confirmed, when the son I'd never heard a curse word out of, looked me directly in the eye and said scathingly "What the Hell are you doing here? Mom, you're embarrassing me, you're not supposed to be down here!"

"The coach asked me to come down to make sure you're OK." I defended myself as Peyton glared at me. One of his biggest fears at sixteen wasn't being injured, but being embarrassed by Dad or Mom.

When the coaches asked him questions like "Who's the president of the United States?" to see if he could answer them knowledgeably, Peyton rolled his eyes and spat out, "Duh, George Washington!"

He went back out on the field because he insisted he was fine, only to have the quarterback call a time out from the huddle, take my son by the arm and walk him back to the sidelines. Our boy, who lived and breathed football, couldn't remember how to execute his favorite play.

We did what we thought was the right thing and got him checked out at the local ER and then took him home and watched over him for a couple days until he seemed to act "normal" again. We let him go back out on the field like so many other parents do with their athletic children, as soon as we felt he was OK. We didn't connect, at the time that he began having migraines, or that maybe, just maybe, there should have been something in place that stops athletes from going back out on the field too soon and risking a second and possible permanent injury. I mean, for goodness sake, "It's just a concussion."

We were lucky. Peyton continued to play football, broke school records for rushing yards and got to live out his dream, at sixteen, to be the best running back on his team. Other than the occasional migraine, he didn't seem to suffer any long term effects. He did eventually tell me that he answered the president question on the field that way because he really couldn't remember who was president and didn't want the coaches to know.

A year later, I got to experience first hand what a concussion felt like too when my car was rear-ended by a truck, while I was stopped for a school bus letting out children. I didn't go to the hospital. I just remember waking up from a strange blackness with my head on the steering wheel and thinking; "Oh, my head hurts." I don't even think I consciously thought about being knocked out because as soon as I regained consciousness, my only thought was "What damage was done to my car?"

While giving the reports to the trooper a little later, I vaguely remember telling him what happened. I think I answered all his questions intelligently, but in all honesty, I don't remember and I don't even think I mentioned that my head hurt. I remember waking up the next day feeling really fuzzy headed, like a heavy curtain of fog was dropped around my head and I had to try to hear, see and think through the thickness. I couldn't concentrate on anything because I had a whopping headache. My head felt like it weighed fifty pounds making it almost impossible for my neck to hold it upright.

I went to the chiropractor a couple days later because Dave kept insisting I see a doctor and finally wore me down. I was treated for whip lash and remember discussing how my head felt. It was then that the word "concussion" was again used and my first thought after that was; "Ahh, so this is what Peyton felt like."

It took me a little longer to recover and it came in stages. I remember waking up in the morning and not feeling that fuzzy thickness and thinking "Oh good, I can get this done and this done and this," making a mental list of everything I'd forgotten to do the day before. Then, in two hours, the fog would return leaving me helpless not even able to remember that I had a list. I didn't have a choice but to lie down on the couch from exhaustion by noon wishing this thick fuzzy feeling in my head would just go away so I could think again.

I did really embarrassing things. About a week after my accident, I was picking the boys up from football practice. I stopped at the local chain restaurant because teenage boys are always starving. I ordered the food at the drive thru window, handed the girl my money and drove away. Luckily before I got out of the parking lot my very hungry boys reminded me that food would be nice, so I drove back around to the front of the restaurant and sheepishly walked inside where the girl behind the register smirked and handed me my food.

It was so embarrassing to ask someone to repeat what they just said to me because I couldn't understand it. I remember friends and family jokingly making comments that my "elevator didn't go all the way to the top". At the time I didn't even understand what that meant so I laughed along with them not understanding the implications. Not once during that time of recovery did I realize my actions were strange. I might be confused or embarrassed over something I attempted to say or do, and failed at, because I could remember that I could do the same thing months ago. My brain just didn't allow me to process that next step or to understand I was really injured.

Luckily again, after a couple months, I recovered, like my son, and could even joke about the silly things we had done after our concussions. 85% of the people that sustain concussions go through very similar circumstances, possibly not even going to the emergency room, because with a head injury it's so often just termed "got their bell rung," or "it's just a concussion." It's not that big of a deal really, we all know someone in our lives who has had some type of concussion and after all, they got over it. It's just a natural assumption that everyone does.

September 25, 2006 changed all of that for our family when our youngest child Elizabeth (known to her friends as Libby) was involved in a school bus accident. It was considered a minor accident that happened in the school bus loop. Libby's bus was about to enter the street that the bus loop starts and ends at, when a teacher flagged the bus down, running across the grass in the center of the circle with a little girl who was about to miss the bus. So naturally Libby's bus driver stopped. Here's the catch, though. Normally when entering the street, even though there is a stop sign at the end of the bus loop, the busses are directed into traffic by a crossing guard. It's one continuous line rolling along, then splitting left or right when turning on to the street. So when Libby's bus stopped, they broke the routine of not stopping. The driver behind them was preoccupied by students and didn't see that the bus in front of him had come to a halt. Before he had time to react, he hit Libby's bus and sent it out into the street. The rear of Libby's bus barely showed damage except for a cracked window and bent bumper, but the front end of the bus that ran into hers had damage. The grill was smashed and radiator fluid spilled out onto the ground.

Libby's normal seat was the very back seat on the passenger side and it just happened that was where the bus hit, sending her head snapping backwards, then forward. She hit the back of her head on the seat she was sitting in and then flew forward, hitting her forehead on the bar encased seat in front of her.

I received a call from the school within a half hour after the accident occurred letting me know that Libby's bus would be delayed because there had been a minor accident at school. They had to wait for another bus to load the kids on and take them home. I was assured that everyone was fine, but something in the woman's voice sent warning bells off in my head. For the next hour I paced, glancing out the window, and then wandering into the kitchen, puttering, staying busy and making coffee I didn't really want to drink. I finally called my mother just to pass the time until the bus arrived home.

I am a worry wart by nature and, if given enough time, my imagination can picture the worst. I've learned through the years that sitting and thinking about what might be, does me no good and I've learned to put those worries out of my head by staying busy or doing something that takes my mind off those doomsday thoughts.

I finally heard the bus as it slowed to a stop, more than an hour later than usual. As soon as Libby got inside, I knew that, this time my worries hadn't been unfounded. Something was definitely wrong. She was pale, hunched over, wouldn't look at me and wouldn't answer questions but went to the nearest chair and gingerly sat down; resting her elbows on the arms and cradling her head in the palm of her hands. Her long dark brown hair fell around her hands and covered her face, hiding her expression. I knelt down in front of her and placed my hand on her wrist. I tried asking questions while she moaned and gave noncommittal, guttural answers.

"Libby, did anyone check you out to see if you were ok?" I asked. The paleness of her skin frightened me. "Honey, talk to me. I need to find out where you hurt. Did anyone check on you?"

"The nurse, but she said I was fine," Libby finally whispered. "Oh and Trooper John asked me questions, but I think I gave him the wrong answers." She moaned again and was silent for a few seconds.

"Am I thirteen, or fourteen?" she asked, looking up finally. Her big brown eyes were so filled with pain they looked almost black in color.

That's all I needed to hear. It was my signal that said to head for the emergency room. I called my husband Dave, quickly filled him in and helped Libby to the car. Dave drove straight from work and met us at the hospital within the hour.

Once we arrived at the emergency room and talked to the receptionist, she explained that Libby would have to wait in the waiting room. They seemed very busy and the waiting room was almost full too. Every few minutes a nurse would open the door to the waiting area, glance around the room, and then disappear again.

As I looked around, I realized that the faces were familiar. They were other students from Libby's bus, so I wasn't the only concerned parent bringing a child in from the accident.

We sat in the waiting room for only a few minutes when a nurse looked out and saw Libby's distress. Libby wouldn't stop moaning or sit still. She'd try to lean her head on me for a few seconds, then moan and bend over in her chair holding her head in her hands. The nurse came over and asked me a couple questions about Libby's condition. I told her she'd been complaining of head, neck and back pain.

We were immediately escorted back to a curtained room as the nurse shouted orders. "This child needs to be looked at immediately, she has a head injury!" There was a flurry of activity as Libby was placed on a back board and a collar was placed around her neck, immobilizing her.

Libby did several things in the emergency room that concerned me. She didn't remember the doctor who looked at her even though he'd been her pediatrician when she was small and had treated her in the ER several times for sprains and stitches. They had a standing joke between them every time they saw each other. When Libby was two, she used to take the stethoscope from around the doctor's neck and put it to her ears telling him she wanted to hear his heart beep. Whenever they would meet he'd ask her "Want to hear my heart beep today?" Libby also swallowed a penny when she was two years old and this doctor had treated her for that. He nicknamed her "Piggy Bank".

He had a charming English accent, and a couple times Libby commented that he talked funny when he was examining her. I explained that he was English.

"Don't you remember? He's the doctor that stitched your face and put a cast on your hand." Libby didn't have a clue.

"She doesn't remember you," I whispered to the doctor.

"That's ok, Mum; I'm not really all that memorable." I noticed after my comment he paid closer attention to her, even though he continued to reassure me that her actions were completely normal for what she'd been through.

Libby did the opposite of what the doctor and nurses asked her to do. If they said "Hold still," she'd move, trying to sit up, pulling against the restraints they had placed around her. Several times Libby tried to remove her neck brace, but the nurse would take her hands and in a calm demeanor, reassure Libby that she needed her to be still.

The hospital staff was wonderful to us, but one nurse in particular came into our room and said, "I don't know about you Mom, but if I were you, I'd be really upset. The school handled this all wrong. They could have called us in advance and we could have had a triage set up and ready for these kids. This was just wrong!"

I nodded in agreement, but at that moment my main concern was for my daughter. It did plant that seed, causing me to wonder a little later; why the school hadn't noticed what I thought was Libby's obvious distress. Why hadn't they called for EMT's? Our small community hospital was full of students, all from the accident. The girl who had been seated in the other back seat was in the cubby next to us and she too had a neck brace and was strapped to a back board just like Libby.

They observed Libby for several hours and after the X-rays came back negative and her pain had been slightly relieved with pain killers, Libby was released to go home. Of course we were told if we had any concerns, to contact her regular physician but they felt it was just a concussion.

And that was that. No ambulance, nobody really thinking anything other than like Dave, Peyton and myself, she'd recover in a couple days. She never lost consciousness, wasn't in a coma. She didn't even have to spend the night in the hospital.

I'd seen what my son looked like and knew how I'd felt, but this just seemed different. I could look into Libby's eyes and see that she didn't really comprehend. She was slightly detached from reality, but I listened to the doctor, took her home and tried to get her to bed to rest. It didn't feel right.

On the way home, Libby became very upset because she had done poorly on a Biology test. She was to retake the test the following day giving her the chance for a better grade, and was angry that she'd spent the entire evening in the hospital when she should have been studying and doing homework.

"Libby, I think the teachers will understand…"

"Mom, you don't get it, I have to retake that test tomorrow and now I've blown it cause' I couldn't study."

"Honey, I'm sure if we talk to the teacher, she will reschedule the test for you another time…"

"Ugh…, we can only take the test the next day. She won't let me. I've blown it. Now I'm gonna have to take a seventy two and I won't make honor roll."

Libby continued to argue as I tried a few other suggestions. Finally I gave up. This conversation was upsetting her and she needed to stay calm. By the time we got home Libby was exhausted and in tears. I walked her to her bed, found her favorite jammies, helped her into them and tucked her in.

"Mom, will you sleep with me tonight? I don't want to be alone and I really hurt all over." Her brown eyes, usually so sunny, were brimming with tears.

"Of course, Honey, I need to keep an eye on you anyway. Just let me go get my nightie on and I'll be right back."

I was relieved she'd asked because, at fourteen, Libby was in that stage between childhood and womanhood and I never knew whether my little girl or this almost-woman would appear, hugging me one minute or the next acting as if I had leprosy. Tonight, I just wanted to be close and watch over her.

I called my cousin on the way to my bedroom. Her little girl rode Libby's bus and I just wanted to make sure that Kaitlin was OK. The conversation only took a couple minutes, with my cousin reassuring me that Kaitlin was fine, but Sherry was upset that no one had called her to let her know that the busses would be late. Then I knew. If they called me and not Sherry, they must have known about Libby's injuries.

Libby was a tough, athletic girl and had had her share of minor injuries. She grew up on our horse farm and when she was nine, was bitten on the cheek by one of our horses. The injury required eight stitches. While I worried that the scar would embarrass her and be a constant reminder of the bite, Libby came home from school the next day all smiles telling me how the boys thought it was *awesome* that she had stitches. She seldom over reacted to pain, but usually thought stitches and casts were pretty cool, and wore them as badges of honor. I just couldn't convince myself that she was really OK this time because her actions in the hospital and in the car were so out of character for our usually happy-go-lucky daughter.

Don't get me wrong, there were tears and drama as the stitches were sewn and the exams on broken fingers and toes took place, but once the cast was on and the stitching done, Libby's eyes would light up with relief and she would be back to her chatty, bubbly self. She would be ready to show off that new accessory at school the next day.

This person in front of me, eyes filled with pain and tears, was a daughter I wasn't used to seeing. I crawled into bed and snuggled up against her back; put my arm around her in comfort. I spent the rest of the night sleeplessly listening to her breath, offered her ice packs for her neck if she moaned, or more Ibuprofen when she complained.

As I lay there, I thought about the phone conversation I'd had with the woman from the school. This woman seemed to hesitate just a few seconds too long when I asked if everyone was OK. She stumbled over her words as she tried to reassure me that Libby was fine. Why hadn't they sent her to the hospital? Why hadn't they at least called EMT's? Why had they sent her home or worse, made her wait on the bus for over an hour while they brought another bus around to finish delivering the kids home? I had a lot of questions that I planned on getting answers to when I called the school the next day.

CHAPTER 2

Us

I should back up and tell you a bit about Libby and our family. Libby was our last child (yes, the baby) and our little surprise, but a very welcome one. Our two sons, Peyton and Tony were already eleven and thirteen when we found we were expecting another child. Once Dave and I got over the shock, and yes, the boys' embarrassment that their parents still "did that," we were overjoyed to be adding to our family.

Secretly I prayed for a girl when I found out I was having another baby. I grew up with three sisters and spent the last fifteen years living in a testosterone filled house with no one who wanted to go shopping, get their hair done, or look at women's magazines. It was all football and outdoors and tractors.

The closest my guys got to fashion was ogling some model in a bikini, while Dave whispered suggestively, "Why don't you wear something like that?"

The boys would respond with "Ugh, gross, Dad, she's a Mom," followed by snickers and elbow poking as my two boys avoided eye contact with me.

It would be nice to go to the mall and shop for girly things with pink and lace and frills. I envisioned my daughter and myself years later sharing secrets and giggling over things only women understand. So when Libby arrived, all 9 lb. 10 oz. of her, with loads of dark hair, oh so kissable cheeks, and those huge brown eyes that just melted my heart, yes, I can honestly say I was thrilled. Our life couldn't get better, I thought. Not only did I have my baby girl, she also slept through the night right home from the hospital, rarely cried, and had everyone wrapped around those chubby, baby girl fingers within days.

We'd bought fifty acres a few years before that was an old run down farm and spent a couple years taking down buildings, tearing down old fences and putting up new barns and fences. We started building a basement where we were planning on building our dream house, a log home. Within months, we started a small horse business and were boarding horses with the dream of filling our barn with our own breeding stock some day.

By the time Libby was born, we had five of our own horses and had been showing quarter horses for a couple years. She grew up around horses and the country and hay season and show season. In between the seasons and smell of fresh cut hay and horses I made sure that Libby was also exposed to the feminine side of life. On our days off I'd pack the stroller into the car, and off we'd go to the mall to look at all the "pretties" as Libby called them. As she grew older the mall days were termed "Mother, Daughter Days."

When she was two, we began building our log home and changed horse breeds from quarter horses to Haflingers. Libby was fearless in the barn and thank God Haflingers are gentle creatures. Libby would toddle into the barn, directly up to a horse I was grooming in the aisle and stop under the horse's chin patting its chest saying "Horsey". The mare's eyes would soften and she would gently lower her head to sniff Libby's hair.

Libby would giggle and say "They love me," while the mare made snuffling sounds and wiggled her lips, making a mess of tangles in the top of Libby's head.

By the time she was four, Libby showed her first horse at the county fair. She'd watched me in the ring and insisted that she be allowed to try, so off she went leading her mare Mable, running towards the judge with a huge smile on her face. I watched the judges eyes grow huge as this tiny girl fearlessly ran up to him towing an eight hundred pound horse. The smile was just as big on his face as I heard my daughter firmly call "WHOA" and both Libby and Mable came to a halt just a few short steps from the man. They got a 2nd place ribbon the first time in the ring.

At seven, Libby and Mable placed in the youth divisions at our National Haflinger Show. Libby got an 8th place ribbon and was the youngest in the group of twenty two, with ages ranging from seven to eighteen years. By then we owned close to twenty Haflingers. Libby grew up in the barn, knew where baby horses came from and was a real animal person. She was good at school, but, at times, could be that typical pre-teen who had attitude and thought the world revolved around her. At the same time, she also understood what hard work can accomplish.

My husband Dave was a foreman for a road construction company. In the summer he was gone at daybreak and back home at dark, usually exhausted, so the farm work fell on our shoulders. Eventually we joined partnerships with Dave's Mom and Dad who considered themselves snowbirds. Dad had retired, sold their home in the Buffalo suburbs and was bored already. They bought a motor home and happily sped off to Florida before the first snowfall and then back to our farm for the rest of the year. We leveled off a section of the yard below our barns and every spring they would move in with their motor home and stay until the leaves turned.

Our boys would help clean pens, switch horses to their proper pasture for the day and on occasion, I could coax Tony into a show ring. In reality neither boy cared much for the farm. Peyton was all about football and girls. Tony, though he loved the farm equipment, really didn't like horses. Libby seemed to be the only child who had any interest in the farm. She was always in the middle of whatever we were doing, whether it was filling our barn with hay, or sitting in the buggy as I worked horses instead of playing dolls or dress up. Her favorite toy was a miniature grooming kit we'd found at a tack shop.

To our surprise in 4th grade, Libby wanted to learn to play the violin. For two years we wondered if that was such a good idea as we listened to screeching bows and almost recognizable versions of "Twinkle, Twinkle", "Go Tell Aunt Rhody", and an occasional classical piece. In 7th grade Libby finally decided to take her music seriously and by the end of that school year she'd actually become a violinist we enjoyed listening to.

She was more interested in classical music than punk rock, which thrilled us. We'd already lived through two sons who blasted Smashing Pumpkins, Guns and Roses and whatever Metallica tape they could get their hands on, so to hear Mozart and Bach on the radio and learn that our daughter not only knew the composer but the name of the Sonata was a welcome change.

When Libby was thirteen, because she worked so hard, we decided to let Mable have a foal and rather than sell the foal, give it to Libby. She could keep it or sell it, whichever she decided, but the upkeep of the foal would be her responsibility. She was thrilled and spent the next year mothering her mare, making sure she was healthy and happy in preparation for the new baby.

She also continued with her violin even though her teachers played musical schools. In 8th grade Mr. Michaels, Libby's favorite music teacher, was moved to the high school to teach. Her grade school orchestra teacher now had double duty at the junior high too. Libby was a little disappointed to find that Mr. Michaels was being moved, not that the other teacher wasn't a good teacher. She was a nice woman and a very good teacher, but it had been Mr. Michaels who encouraged Libby to go further with her music. He had been hired fresh out of college, with new ideas, loads of energy and just wouldn't give up on his students. He would hound Libby to practice, even going so far as to tape a picture of himself on her violin with the words *PRACTICE* written below.

During 8th grade Libby continued to advance in her music and was even asked by Mr. Michaels to play with the senior high orchestra for graduation ceremonies that year. During practice Mr. Michaels came to me amazed at how far she'd come since his transfer to the high school, and a little concerned that when she moved up to the high school next year, her abilities may be beyond what he could teach. In college he hadn't majored in violin, but in bass and encouraged us to find someone who would help keep Libby playing at her own pace. He told us that she had real talent so we decided private lessons were in order. We found a private teacher in a nearby town.

Libby was such a combination of tomboy and girly girl; we never knew who would be walking out of her room. One minute she'd be out the door to check on her horses or a new batch of kittens and the next she'd be playing Bach, or Mozart. She could easily compete in burping contests with her brothers or spend hours looking up music colleges telling everyone in the family she was going to Eastman, or Julliard, and that she dreamed of traveling the world, playing her music.

When her foal was born, she naturally named him "Mozart" and would spend hours in his stall, sitting in the straw, while mom and baby rustled around. I'm convinced that her mare, Mable, just thought she was another part of the herd, because one day I found Libby asleep in the stall, with her arms curled around Mozart. He was stretched out snoozing away without a care in the world and Mable was standing over both, calmly munching hay with that dreamy "contented Mothers" look in her eyes.

Libby was never what you would consider a delicate girl, but she was beautiful. She hated her hands which were nicely shaped but large. She wore a size nine shoe by the time she was thirteen. She was well muscled from her farm chores and had an athletic build. She had gorgeous thick brown hair that was usually pulled back in a pony tail and huge dark brown eyes that showed every emotion clearly. She was naturally a happy child who just went where we went, did what we did and never complained, always with a smile on her face.

Occasionally, when Libby was younger, she would wrap her arms around me and snuggle her nose deep into my neck, taking a deep breath. "Hmm, Mommy," she would say contentedly. As she grew older she did that less and less, but occasionally, I'd still feel that nose deep in my neck and treasure what I knew was coming next.

We encouraged her to expand beyond the farm. She did a little, occasionally trying out different sports, but most of the time, she was pretty content to just come home and be with her horses and practice her violin. Libby had quite a few friends and they always liked coming to the farm. Libby was the only friend that had horses and they could ride all over the fields. Our house was usually full of giggling girls, which, of course, drove her brothers crazy. For a while I think both boys avoided our house like the plague.

In early September of 2006, she auditioned for a youth orchestra, in a city over an hour away from us, and was accepted. It was quite a drive for us, but such an opportunity for Libby that we happily gave up our Sundays. We were so proud. It seemed she would be our easy child. She had a good head on her shoulders, already knew what she wanted, of course, after going through all the ballerina, veterinarian, and yes even princess when she was six, all the typical girl dreams.

Her grades weren't straight A, but she had a good steady B+. On occasion her grades would slip a little because she was such a social butterfly. At times, friends and boys were much more important than good grades, but once she set her sights on a music college and becoming a music teacher, she took her school work seriously and we noticed a great improvement in her grades by the end of 8th grade.

Libby told us that her goal in 9th grade was to be high honor roll all the way through, because now she'd be in high school and that's when the grades really counted for college. We never had to remind her to do homework, she just did it. So naturally, after her accident, her main concern was her poor Biology grade and how she could get that grade up.

She'd just moved up from the junior high into the high school and was excited because she was now considered one of the big kids. She was a little nervous at first about finding her way around, but by the end of the first day in high school, Libby bounced through our door excited because her teachers all seemed "cool," she'd only gotten lost once, and wonder of wonders, Mr. Michaels was her orchestra teacher again.

She started out her freshman year with a bang, bringing home high nineties on all of her papers, until she'd gotten a seventy two on her Biology test. Libby was determined to bring that grade up to at least a ninety and planned on studying all evening so she could retake the test the next day.

CHAPTER 3

Day 2 and...

Before Libby woke the next morning, I spent an hour making phone calls. My first one was to our school superintendent Mrs. Crabner. I let her know immediately that I was upset at the way they made Libby sit on the bus for so long, with no medical attention. She assured me that the nurse looked at Libby and felt she was OK enough to send home. I reminded her that a concussion could be serious and if Libby had a brain bleed she could have died because of their lack of attention. I also told her about the other students who were in the ER and that the hospital wasn't at all happy with the school because they hadn't even let them know that kids could possibly be coming in from the accident.

I hung up feeling a little better, but also feeling like I'd just been "handled". Everything Mrs. Crabner said had been so neutral. She hadn't even commented on Libby's injuries when I told her about her diagnosis, but simply said that they'd have to look into their bus policies on accidents, without telling me exactly what those policies were.

Libby came out of her room around 9:00 a.m. looking very pale. "My head's killing me," she whispered squinting at the sunshine streaming through the doorway. She was still pale and had rows of worry lines across her forehead from frowning.

I went to the kitchen, poured her a juice and handed her some Ibuprofen. Libby stared at the pills in her hand and then looked at me.

"Honey, take them. They'll help with your headache." Nothing... she continued to stare at the pills and juice blankly.

"Elizabeth, put the pills in your mouth and swallow them" I said firmly.

She put the pills in her mouth and drank a little of the juice, then continued to stand there saying nothing, so I took the juice from her and set it back on the table in the kitchen.

Again she whispered "My heads killing me. The TV's too loud." She walked over to the remote and picked it up. I waited for her to turn the volume down, but instead she stared at the remote like she had stared at the pills.

Libby looked up at me with such a look of concentration. "I know I'm supposed to do something with this, but I don't know what," she said.

I rushed into the family room, took the remote from her hands and turned down the television. Her face was scrunched up in a scowl, squinting against the brightness of the room. I was glad I'd let her sleep. She was obviously in no shape to go to school. As Libby continued to stand, rooted to one place, I bustled around the windows, closing the curtains against the bright light.

The rest of the morning, I spent watching Libby and compared what I remembered feeling when I had my concussion. When Libby couldn't remember how to run the remote I remembered sitting down at my keyboard, getting ready to type a newsletter for our Haflinger registry, and just staring at the keyboard, knowing that I knew how to type, but for the life of me, I couldn't remember where to put my fingers, or what I should do next.

Libby spent the morning alternating between lying down being very quiet to getting highly agitated when she was up and walking around. She kept insisting that she needed to go to school and get her homework, so she wouldn't fall behind, and if I tried to talk to her and tell her it could wait, she became frantic. Obviously, my daughter, who very seldom ever sassed or spoke back to Mom and Dad, was not acting normal and it didn't take me long to realize that saying nothing was better than trying to reassure her and say the wrong thing.

When she was up, she wandered around looking at the things in our house like she'd never seen them before. She walked over to the piano, looked at the sheet music on the stand, put her fingers on the piano keys and… nothing.

Libby stood there for a few moments staring at her fingers and then turned to me and asked. "Who plays the piano?"

"You do, Honey, I used to when I was younger, but you take lessons now, remember?"

She shook her head no, grimaced slightly from the movement and then glanced back to the sheet music and scowled. Without a word she turned and walked to her bedroom. I followed her and as I reached the doorway I saw Libby standing over her violin case.

"I play this, right?"

"Yes, you play the violin beautifully."

"I think I remember."

Libby took the violin out of its case, pulled out some sheet music that she'd been practicing on that week, tightened the horsehair on her bow and played. The notes were true, though weak. She looked up at me with such wonder.

"Wow, I really can play!"

"Yes, Honey, you really can." I smiled back at her even though my stomach was doing flip flops. How could she not know that she played violin well?

She walked back out to the piano and studied that again for several seconds, shook her head back and forth slowly, shrugged and said "Nope, don't remember." She walked back into her room and lay down on her bed without saying another word.

"I think I better call her piano teacher and let her know that lessons are out for a while." I thought to myself after watching Libby.

It got quiet in her room, so I tiptoed around the kitchen, picking up, hoping she had fallen asleep. Ten minutes later she came back out to the kitchen, restless again.

"I can't sleep, I hurt too much." She reached her right hand up and cupped her chin with it supporting the weight of her head in her hand.

"Libby, you really should try to rest, that's what's really going to make you feel better."

"Mom, I said it hurts too much I can't!" Libby raised her voice scrunching her shoulders

"Ok, you don't have to lie down."

"I just said I can't lie down, it hurts too much!"

"I know, Honey, its OK; you don't have to lie down. What would make you feel better?"

"I already told you, I have to go to school. If I don't go, I'll fall behind and I know I messed up now, on my test, cause' I'm going to miss the retake."

At this point, she'd raised her voice enough that she was cringing in pain and holding on to her head with both hands. I had to diffuse this situation, but I didn't know what to do.

"I really don't think you should go, you can just rest today and if you feel better tomorrow, we'll see." I put a hand on her arm hoping to guide her to the nearest chair, but she jerked away and looked at me with pure panic in her eyes.

"Mom, you don't get it. I have to go to school. I have to tell Mrs. Floorz that I can't take the test, and I have to get my homework."

"If I take you down to the school, and you get your homework, will you promise me you'll rest when we get home and try to sleep?"

Libby was so disconcerted that she didn't have her work, there was no consoling her. It didn't make sense. She should be in bed resting, but I couldn't keep her there. It was awful to watch her pace, hold on to her head, moan, disappear into her room and then come back out and repeat our school conversation. I finally decided I'd drive her down to school, hoping if she got this off her chest or out of her thoughts, she'd be able to settle down.

As soon as we were in the car, she calmed down and even closed her eyes for a few minutes. When I pulled up in front of the school and shut the car off, Libby opened her door and got out, took a few steps and stopped. She looked around at the school building in front of her and asked.

"Where are we?"

"Oh my God," I thought. "She's got to be joking." One look at her face told me she wasn't, so as calmly as I could, I said, "You're at school."

Without another word she walked to the doors and opened them and walked in, but once inside she stopped again and looked at me in a panic.

"I don't know where I am."

"You're at the high school, remember?" That sinking feeling in the pit of my stomach was growing. "Do you want to go back to the car?"

She shook her head no. I had no idea what to do. This was a mistake, I should never have given in and brought her down here, but here we were standing in the hallway with me trying to think how I could just get her home and settled down, and Libby, even though she didn't know where she was, determined to stay.

"Do you want to go to the guidance office? Maybe they can get your homework for you." Standing here was getting us nowhere and my mind was racing, trying to come up with something that would help Libby.

Libby nodded her head, so I took her by the arm and walked her the short distance down the hall to the guidance office, all the while mentally kicking myself for letting her out of the house. This was so surreal.

Once in the office, I quietly explained to the secretary that Libby had a concussion and was having trouble remembering things, but wanted her homework.

The secretary looked at me, and then at Libby. With a slight scowl she asked her. "Do you want to go to your locker and get your books and I'll call around to the teachers?"

Libby nodded yes and started for the door, but stopped just short of opening it. She turned back to the secretary. "I don't know where my locker is." Surprise registered on the secretary's face.

A boy in Libby's grade walked into Guidance and thinking fast, the secretary asked him if he could show her to her locker. I asked Libby if she knew what her combination was and she said "no", so the secretary wrote it down for us. Jeff, the student, looked at Libby, me and the secretary suspiciously. I explained to him that Libby had a concussion and had lost her memory, but wanted her books. He looked at her warily, but agreed to take her to her locker. I didn't even ask, but followed, because at this point I had no idea what would happen next or what she'd remember or not remember.

I was starting to feel like a broken record. "Libby can't remember, she has a concussion…Libby can't remember…she has a concussion."

Libby whispered to me. "Do I know that kid?"

"Yes," I murmured back. "It's either Jeff or his twin brother Jason." I knew him well enough to know he had an identical twin and it was almost impossible to tell them apart.

He mumbled, looking over his shoulder at us. "I'm Jeff."

"Do you know where my locker is?"

"Yea, it's close to mine." He led us up the stairs and down the hallway.

"Do you know where Biology is? Can you take me to Bio? I have to tell Mrs. Floorz I can't take a test." Libby rattled on absently.

The scowl on his face said it all. He'd known Libby since kindergarten and was looking at her like she was a total stranger, but he took her to her locker and then to Biology without saying a word.

As soon as Libby saw the teacher she tugged at my shirt sleeve and said, "I think that's the teacher. I remember I'm scared of her."

Mrs. Floorz came over to Libby, and Jeff made a hasty exit. Before she had a chance to say anything, I jumped in with my now familiar response and explained that Libby had been on one of the busses, in the accident, the day before, and had a concussion. I was astonished to find that Mrs. Floorz didn't even know there'd been an accident. I told the teacher that Libby's memory seemed to be all jumbled up but she did remember that she was supposed to take a makeup test today. I suggested that under the circumstances possibly Libby could retake the test at a later time? Mrs. Floorz was very understanding and told Libby not to worry about anything, but to go home and rest and she assured her that she'd be able to make up the test once she came back to school. I could see the relief in Libby's eyes and thanked Mrs. Floorz and we left.

Once in the hallway, Libby remembered orchestra and wanted to go there, so I took her to the orchestra room. It was empty, except for Mr. Michaels. While she wandered around the room, I told him about Libby's concussion. Again, shock to find he didn't know about the accident either. He gave Libby a hug and told her to go home and rest. She nodded her head in agreement. Libby's color was very pale and I could see she was running out of steam fast.

We headed down the hallway to the front door. On the way, two of Libby's girl friends saw her and ran up asking her where she'd been all morning. Libby didn't answer them but just looked at me with that panic look on her face again. I explained to the two girls that she'd been in an accident and didn't remember things.

Both girls looked surprised, and at the same time asked, "Do you remember me?" Libby shook her head no.

"Wow," one girl said. "You must have really got your bell rung."

Not waiting for Libby to answer Angela hugged her and said "I hope you remember us soon, cause' that would suck if you didn't." Angie and Tiffany raced down the hallway, calling back that they were late for class.

"Are they my friends?" She asked as she watched the girls' race away.

"Yes, Honey, they are, they both came to your Halloween party last year and spent the night." She didn't answer. I took her arm and guided her down the hall, quickly grabbed her homework from guidance, and got her out to the car. I could see she was exhausted, but at least she wasn't frantic anymore. Maybe now she could go home and rest.

A few minutes later Libby looked at me with tears in her eyes and asked. "Do I only have two friends?"

"No, Honey, you have lots of friends. Why?"

"Cause I can only remember two. Janine and some other girl, but I can't think of her name. I think its Kiara."

"Janine is one of your best friends and Kiara's your cousin." I reminded her gently.

"Oh, I thought she was a friend." Libby's chin quivered.

I named off about a dozen kids that I knew, hoping she'd settle down again and this time it worked. I think, really, she was just too exhausted to do anything else. I was scared though. No concussion I'd ever seen or experienced ever had this much memory loss. There was so much missing from her memory, already, just from what I'd seen happen this morning.

As soon as I got home and got Libby in bed, I called our family doctors' office, only to find she wasn't in that day, but they could see her on Friday. That was two days away. I didn't want to wait that long. So after Libby woke up several hours later and did a few more things like picking up the phone to call her cousin and then not knowing how to dial the phone or what to do with it, just like the remote earlier that day, I made the decision to take her back to the emergency room and have someone check her again.

She'd also shown signs of not understanding what I was saying to her because I had to repeat things, or change the words until she understood. She had, several times that day, in agitation, told me to talk slower; I was making her head hurt. When Libby did talk, she was beginning to stumble over words. I noticed, as the day wore on, it was getting worse and she would just shrug, give a slight shake to her head and go silent rather than finish what she was trying to say.

What scared me the most, though, was when Libby took out her English homework, determined to work on a book report.

I sat down and picked up a book to read, but noticed she was fidgeting and scowling as she wrote. When I looked at the writing, I was shocked. I could barely read what she had written. The words were incomplete, letters were written backwards and there were no suffixes or prefixes on anything.

"Does it look OK?" Libby asked innocently.

What do I tell her? By the look on her face, I can tell she has no idea what she's just done. I opted for the easy way out because I just didn't know what else to do.

"Honey, why don't you put your work up for now? I'll help you with it a little later."

I called Dave and told him about the morning and Libby's writing. He agreed that we shouldn't wait until Friday to see a doctor.

"Take her back to the emergency room. I'll meet you there as soon as I'm done at work," he said. Today was Dave's birthday, but all thoughts of a celebration were forgotten, as we made the decision to go back to the hospital.

For the second time in twenty four hours, we headed back to the hospital. There was a different doctor on call, so after explaining what I'd seen in Libby's actions and telling the Doctor about the school visit, he ordered a CAT scan. Once the results of that came back clean, he sent her home again, telling us that with a concussion, especially one of this magnitude, memory loss was not uncommon, but not to worry too much. He said to give her a couple days and we'll be amazed at how fast she'll bounce back. He agreed Libby should see her family physician on Friday just to make sure and signed her release papers.

I have to say, I've handled situations of broken bones, torn ACL's, a knee surgery and been fine, but this time I felt I was out of my element. I just didn't know how to help Libby, except to keep her still, which was almost impossible. Someone with a broken bone knows that if you move, you hurt. Someone with a head injury doesn't. My gut told me she should be in a hospital, but at this point I'd had two doctors tell me to take her home and let her rest and she'd be fine.

When Peyton was eleven he was downtown playing with some of his friends at the Recreation Center. One boy about his age was sitting on the railing at the center when the boy lost his balance and fell backwards to the concrete below. He didn't lose consciousness, but cried a little and told Peyton and his buddies his head hurt. The Recreation Center called the boy's parents and they came and picked him up. He walked to the car on his own. The next day we found out that Davy had died. He'd had a subdural hematoma and by the time he showed any real signs of a massive head trauma, it was too late to save him. It's so scary to think that someone who could talk and walk would die within hours, but it happens.

This boy's grave stone sits on the edge of the cemetery overlooking the elementary school and is a reminder to many people in the community how fragile life can be. With only a bump, or some accident that might be considered minor, a life can be cut short, or have devastating results.

When Peyton was hurt, of course I thought of this boy, and when Libby was hurt, I even commented to the superintendent of the school that we'd had a boy die with a brain injury, in our town. It really angered me that they'd dismissed Libby so easily even though she'd told the nurse her head, neck and back hurt, and that she had trouble answering their questions.

This last time, at the hospital, the receptionist questioned me on billing because they thought possibly the schools' insurance would pay Libby's bills, but they weren't sure. Mrs. Crabner wasn't sure when I called her so she had me call the bus garage superintendent, Fred Simmons. He helped us as much as he could by informing us that our New York State No-Fault insurance would be responsible for Libby's medical bills because her accident happened on a municipal bus. I thought that was outrageous. How my own car insurance could be expected to pay bills when my car wasn't even involved in the accident. Within twenty four hours I received the same information from the schools insurance company and my own.

Fred was the only person in authority in our whole school district who even apologized for the accident. Even though it didn't change the fact that she'd been injured, it made such a difference to me. It finally felt like someone cared in our school. Someone cared enough to have answers to our questions and say they were sorry. Instead of feeling handled, I felt helped.

It didn't last long though. By Friday I was beginning to see a pattern. Everything regarding Libby's care would be handled by us and our insurance company, while the school administration began to bury their heads in the sand like ostriches and pretend the accident never happened.

I gave permission to the school superintendent to inform all of Libby's teachers about the accident and that we just didn't know how long she would be out of school. Mrs. Crabner promised she'd contact each teacher and let them know. We eventually learned that no one was notified, or even knew what had happened to her, not even her school nurse (she'd attended the other bus in the accident) until we called or e-mailed them ourselves.

It still amazes me when our small rural community that knows everyone's business within twenty four hours had no idea there'd been an accident at the school and children had actually been hurt. There was such a lack of communication within the school that it took weeks before teachers, secretaries, parents and other students learned about the bus accident that had taken place in our own school parking lot.

I would soon find that the chain of command stopped with whichever person I talked with. I've learned since that, when something happens at the school that may put them in a bad light or could cause problems, the administration actually tells the teachers not to discuss it amongst themselves. I had a teacher tell me that the school actually puts gag orders on certain incidents. When that happens if the teachers are caught talking about the incident, there could be disciplinary action taken against them.

What a crazy policy. I realize that it's used to control gossip, which definitely can be a problem in any place of business that has so many people under one roof, but to forbid someone to discuss a real issue, or to forbid teachers to get together to try to come up with solutions? As a mom I just couldn't understand. Each of Libby's teachers was left in the dark about her condition and abilities because of this policy.

CHAPTER 4

How long do we wait?

Friday began the first of many, many doctor visits for Libby. Her family physician was a lovely woman, kind, compassionate and reassuring to us, when we took Libby in to see her. Dr. Perry explained that with a concussion the brain swells, causing memory loss; but once the swelling receded, we should see a marked difference in our daughter. She said it could take from a couple days to a couple weeks. When we discussed the extent of Libby's amnesia, the doctor felt that possibly letting her go back to school for a couple hours in the morning might help her recover her memory. Dr. Perry ordered a tutor for the afternoon. She wanted to make sure Libby got enough rest, but also felt getting back into her normal routine would encourage healing.

I'd seen Libby try to read and write and knew she has having a lot of trouble, just with the basics. She seemed to be able to read out loud, but couldn't remember what she read. When she wrote, the handwriting was very childish and hadn't improved at all since I watched her trying to write her English report. She couldn't seem to write in complete sentences. Also in the short few days since her accident, Libby seemed to be constantly in either a panic or too quiet. She wouldn't let me out of her sight and continued to beg every night that I sleep with her. Dave and I discussed it and decided that, for a while at least, I'd sleep with her in case she needed anything.

Libby had stopped talking to anyone outside our immediate family and when I asked her why, she said. "Because I'm scared they'll ask me qua …qua…things I can't answer and I'll look dumb."

She was beginning to understand that she wasn't remembering people she should know. Too many strangers were coming up to her and talking to her, but they weren't strangers. They were aunts and cousins and neighbors and friends.

She did want to go back to school, but I wasn't sure how she was going to get around. Who would help her? She had no clue where to go or even who to ask if she got lost. Almost everyone in that building was a stranger to Libby.

When we were finished with the doctor's appointment, we stopped back at the school and I gave the office the prescription for a tutor. The secretary seemed harried and simply shrugged and said she'd do her best, but tutors were on a volunteer basis. She didn't know who they could get that would be willing to travel the eleven miles to our house every day. I was a little surprised at her casual attitude, but didn't respond. I then went across the hall to the nurse's station and talked with her about Libby's concussion.

I explained that Libby didn't know where her classes were or who her friends were so the nurse sent us to Guidance and they arranged for a friend to help her to her first class. They would have other kids in the class help her to her following classes. I mentioned to them that she couldn't even really read or write at this point but that we were hoping coming back would jog her memory. If she couldn't tolerate it and became too stressed, I'd come get her. The secretary in guidance wrote down all Libby's teachers e-mail addresses so I could contact them and I gave mine to Guidance in case any teacher might have a question.

I decided that I wanted Libby to ride the bus to school. I noticed that she seemed hesitant about riding one again. Our way of thinking here at home was *if you fall off the horse you get right back on.* I hoped that riding the bus again would eventually relieve Libby's fears.

Over the weekend, I remembered that we had planned on going to the symphony in the city where Libby's youth orchestra played, but had forgotten all about it since the accident. I'd talked with her violin instructor and explained that Libby wouldn't be at practice that week because she'd been in an accident. Libby overheard us talking about the symphony that evening.

"What symphony?" She asked curious

"Well before you got hurt, we were going to the symphony. They support your youth orchestra," I explained.

"What youth orchestra? What are you guys talking about?" Libby scowled at both Dave and me clearly not remembering.

"The one you belong to. You auditioned a couple weeks ago and were accepted and you've been going to practice. Amber teaches lessons to you every Wednesday remember?"

She looked shocked. "I belong to an orchestra? Wow, am I good?"

I couldn't help it. I laughed. Such an innocent question, but it told so much. She had no idea. She began scowling at me and tears welled up in her eyes.

"What's so funny?" She asked. Libby was completely unaware that she really should know if she was good or not.

I felt horrible because I'd brought on tears again for at least the tenth time that day. Dave and I were still in the process of having the reality of amnesia slapping us in the face every few minutes. We were still learning what she could and couldn't remember, while at the same time waiting every morning just to see if she could do something today she hadn't known how to do the day before. Her memory was so random that we couldn't even fathom what the next thing might be that would rattle our sense of well being. Just going from being confident in our daily surroundings to waiting, holding our breath, just to see what Libby might have forgotten next, was crazy.

Libby and I talked a while. I reassured her that, yes, she was that good. We decided to buy the tickets and go, even though it was last minute. I hoped our tickets wouldn't be in the nose bleed section, but having waited until the last minute, we knew we'd have to take what we could get. More than anything, I was hoping going would jog Libby's memory about playing in the orchestra she belonged to.

Dave and I were falling into a routine of making suggestions and waiting to see Libby's reactions. We were learning fast not to take for granted that a simple question or suggestion would be received in a normal fashion. It was just too bizarre. Everything we took for granted we now had to take a step back and think about. We were learning to just deal with the unforeseen as it happened. I don't know why, but I just kept thinking that if we show her this or that it will stir something inside and she would suddenly say "Oh right, now I remember."

For the first time, Libby seemed excited about something since her accident. So we dressed for the symphony and headed out. Our seats were a God send. Front row center, directly in front of the conductor and the concert cellist during her solos. The sound is definitely better from a distance, but for Libby to be so close and be able to see everything, worked perfectly for us. She never took her eyes off the people on stage, and though we pointed out her conductor for youth orchestra, she didn't recognize him. We hadn't told Mr. Lewis yet of Libby's accident, so when he waved to her and she didn't respond, I noticed he looked a little confused. When the soloist came on stage and sat directly in front of us and began playing, Libby leaned over to me and spoke for the first time.

"Now I really know this is what I want to do," she whispered, never taking her eyes off the cellist. We were so close, we could hear the woman's deep intake of breath as she prepared to play the next measure.

By the end of the concert, Libby was exhausted, but seemed content too. She remembered Amber, her violin teacher, and when we talked with Mr. Lewis after the concert and explained to him what had happened, he patted her on the arm and just gave her his best wishes and said he hoped to see her soon at practice. The conductor of the orchestra came over to us and immediately shook Libby's hand.

"You are a musician," she said looking directly into Libby's eyes.

Libby smiled shyly and nodded and said quietly, "I play violin."

"Well I saw you in the audience and the look on your face told me you loved it. Maybe someday you'll be up there and playing for me!"

Libby smiled the sweetest smile and for a moment I could almost forget what we'd been through the past few days. I could have hugged that woman. It was our first real normal moment in five days.

On the way home from the concert, Libby said that she thought she remembered Mr. Lewis, though not from orchestra. When she played at NYSSMA, (New York State School Music Association) he was her judge and she remembered him telling her to work on her bowing, but not a single memory from the previous month of practices.

Every little thing that Libby remembered had us holding our breath waiting. Waiting for that moment when she'd just snap out of it and tell us "Ahh, now I remember." We waited for this crazy nightmare to be over and for everything to go back to normal. We had no idea how long that wait would turn out to be.

On Monday, Libby started back to school. She got on the bus without a word, just looked at me as if I were sending her out to the wolves to fend for herself, and I felt the same way.

"It's too soon." I whispered to no one. "She's not ready yet." The doctor felt she was, for at least a couple of hours, but I didn't think so. Libby spent the day after the concert in bed and would only get out of bed for a short amount of time and then go lie down again, exhausted. This was only the next day. From the moment I watched her step on the bus, I worried. I tried to keep busy, but couldn't seem to stay on any one project. I found myself walking by the phone time and time again.

At 9:00 a.m., just an hour after school started, the phone rang. It was the school nurse, telling me Libby was there and said her head hurt too much. I asked to speak with Libby and encouraged her to try to go back to class for another hour. If she couldn't handle it I'd come get her at 10:00. She agreed, without a fight, so I asked the nurse to give her some Ibuprofen and call me if she needed anything else. At 10:00 a.m. exactly, the phone rang again and it was the nurse. She said she felt Libby was ready to go home and explained that she'd come into the office in tears. I told her to tell Libby I'd be right there.

As soon as I got to school, I found Libby still in tears and just held her for a minute, trying to calm her down, stroking her long brown hair.

"Shh, it's OK," I whispered and after a couple minutes she gathered her emotions in check and asked to leave. On our way out, I stopped at the office and checked to see if they'd found a tutor yet.

"Nobody answered our request to volunteer, but I'll post it again," the secretary said with a shrug. She knew where we lived because her family had a hunting camp only a mile from our house. "You know it's going to be hard to find someone," she said.

"So what do we do until then? Let Libby fall behind? She's already missed a week of school. She can't read or write and she was only here long enough for two classes. How do we get someone?"

The secretary shrugged and just said "We'll have to wait and see."

The second day of school and the third were very much like the first. My scheduled time to get Libby was at 11:00 a.m., but I'd get a call anywhere from 9:30 to 10:30 saying she was exhausted. I'd run down and get her, check in at the office to see how the search for a tutor was coming and then take her home. As soon as we walked in the door, Libby would silently go to her room and sleep for hours, missing lunch sometimes, often not waking until mid afternoon.

We had another appointment that week with the physician who again reassured us that we just needed to wait and give it time. She prescribed Flexeril, because Libby was having back spasms. It was also supposed to help her neck which would get so tired; she would literally hold her chin up with her hand to support her head. We scheduled another appointment for the following week and went home.

Two weeks had passed since the accident; Libby was back in school for an hour or two every day. She still hadn't regained much of her memory and we still didn't have a tutor. By that Friday I went into school again checked on the tutor situation and was told the same story. Wait and see.

"Wait for what, for my daughter to fall so far behind she'll never catch up? You guys need to find a tutor for her. This is getting ridiculous. If you can't find one within this school district, can't you look outside the district? I don't care what you have to do, but you need to find one." I vented at the secretary.

I was so frustrated. How could there be no tutor? There had to be someone, someplace who was willing. Libby couldn't do the work alone. Her teachers barely knew what was going on or what she could and couldn't do. The school just seemed to shrug it off as if it was no big deal. I'd already asked and been turned down to tutor Libby while they looked for someone. I wanted to scream at them. "You did this to her, now fix it." But I didn't. Instead I walked out of the office, climbed in the car, pulled my cell phone from my purse and called my husband, crying. I always thought of myself as a reasonable woman. Now I found that I wanted to scream in frustration and blame people for what Libby was going through.

"They just don't give a damn." I said to Dave. "Half of them don't even know that their school had an accident and the other half just bury their heads in the sand and pretend it'll go away.

Dave asked for the school number, knowing me so well and said "Leave it to me. I'll shake some trees down there and see if a tutor falls out of one of them."

Later, Dave told me that he had gotten through to the vice principal and had let him know that if they didn't have a tutor by Monday, he'd be down personally and make such a scene they'd wished they'd put a little more effort into finding one.

When I picked Libby up Monday morning and went into the office, the secretary excitedly informed me they'd found a tutor. She wrote the tutors' name and number down on a piece of paper and said call her to make arrangements. Kelly Cornish (our first angel) started tutoring October 11, fifteen days after the accident.

Why is it that Mom's can call and call a school, but when Dad calls, things get done? I guess the bigger question would really be why, if a school is given funding by the state, and it's budgeted into their yearly school allowance, do they not automatically have a tutor on stand-by ready for students when needed? New York schools are given this money for situations such as ours, why did we have to wait?

During those two weeks of waiting, we noticed something else that was beginning to happen. Every time Libby got in the car, she'd be a nervous wreck by the time we got home. Once, a truck with loud mufflers passed us and she screamed and started sobbing. For the half-hour long ride home from the doctors' office, she wouldn't be consoled. Also, if anything loud happened near her, she'd startle and begin crying. At school, someone dropped a book in class and that was the end of Libby's day. She had to go to the nurse and wouldn't stop crying until I got there. It killed Dave and me to watch our daughter, who a month ago was all smiles and nothing bothered her, turn into this meek, tearful child we didn't know.

As parents we found our style of parenting ceased as we knew it. We were now turning into people who spoke quietly, whispered, answered questions in soothing voices, and made room for our daughter on the couch next to us every time we sat down. We'd just started getting used to her spending most of her time in her room and now she was where I was, unless she was sleeping.

If I got up to go into the kitchen, she panicked and asked me where I was going and I gently explained, "I just need a drink, I'll be right back."

If Libby did something wrong before the accident, we let her know, not necessarily yelling at her, but letting her know firmly that whatever she'd done was unacceptable and if it happened again, she'd be punished. Our punishments for her were usually grounding, or taking her phone away, or no TV. Rarely did we have to go beyond a warning. Now Libby didn't even seem to understand what right and wrong was. She was in such a survival mode that she spoke what ever came to her mind, not thinking it may hurt someone's feelings.

She might say. "I don't want to watch that TV show." and get up and turn the television off, regardless if others were watching.

In the past, that would have gotten a shout from Dad. "Turn that back on I was watching!"

Now, our reaction was to look at each other as she walked away, with surprise on our faces. "Let's go upstairs and watch in the bedroom," I suggested.

So we stood up and started up the stairs, only to have Libby come out of her room and panic. "Where are you going Mom? Aren't you sleeping with me?"

This would then lead to Dave and me looking at each other in resignation, me shrugging and going back down the stairs to spend another sleepless night in my daughters' room. On rare occasions, she'd fall asleep before we turned off the TV for the night and I'd sneak upstairs to my own bed. Once in a while, I could actually spend the entire night there. More often than not, I would hear her panicky call to me in the dark.

What I didn't know at the time was that Libby was experiencing PTSD, (Post Traumatic Stress Disorder) and was having repeated nightmares of the accident. In her dreams, she was always sitting in the back seat, right where she'd actually been sitting. She could see the bus coming towards her. Sometimes she tried to get her bus drivers' attention, but he wouldn't or didn't see her. Once when the bus hit, the drivers' head fell off. Other times Libby's nieces and nephews would be on the bus and even though she wouldn't get hurt, they would. Sometimes they would have horrible injuries, sometimes they would die and she would see it all in her dreams.

On our next visit, Dr. Perry told us what PTSD was and that it sounded like Libby was experiencing it. She prescribed Zoloft, an anti anxiety drug, hoping that would help. Also at this point,

Dr. Perry decided that Libby's amnesia was still very extensive and that it was time for a second opinion. She referred us to Dr. Marsha Jenkins, a neurologist, still saying that time would be what would heal our daughter, and that sometimes it just takes a little longer with some people.

So now we had a tutor, a family physician and a neurologist. Things were beginning to get done. Somehow it didn't make me feel better. I really wanted answers to why Libby had such extensive amnesia and why she couldn't read and write. Why was she starting to ask me "What does that word mean?" about twenty times a day, simple words that she had known when she was seven and eight. Why hadn't anyone told her teachers what to expect, and why was the school acting like nothing had happened? Why couldn't I sleep with my husband anymore? Why was my daughter white knuckling every car ride now and why and why and why? Every time I asked these questions my answers were "Just wait, just give it time, by next week things will have improved, you'll see.

I found myself talking to people at the school, telling them what we were going through and getting strange looks from them. Did they not believe us? How could they not believe what was obviously in front of their noses? That was the reaction we got from almost everyone except Libby's doctor .The frustration of all of this was unbelievable for me, and I realize now that waiting is not what I do best. I wanted answers and we weren't getting any. It felt as if no one was hearing what we were saying or really saw what we were going through. I'd stopped thinking of this as Libby's injury alone. This injury took hold and absorbed our whole family's attention. Still we had no answers to our questions.

MY DAUGHTER CAN'T REMEMBER SHE TOOK ALGEBRA AND SPANISH LAST YEAR. MY DAUGHTER CAN'T REMEMBER IF SHE'S GOOD WHEN SHE PLAYS HER VIOLIN. WHY CAN SHE READ THE MUSIC NOTES AND UNDERSTAND THEM FOR VIOLIN BUT NOT PIANO?

MY DAUGHER DOESN'T THINK SHE HAS ANY FRIENDS BECAUSE SHE CAN'T REMEMBER THEM. MY DAUGHTER'S HAVING HORRIBLE NIGHTMARES. MY DAUGHTER WON'T LEAVE MY SIDE. MY DAUGHTER CRIES ALL THE TIME. MY DAUGHTER'S HEAD HURTS SO BAD SHE HAS TO HOLD IT IN HER HANDS AND DOESN'T HAVE THE STRENGTH TO KEEP HER OWN HEAD UPRIGHT.

Just wait, it'll get better. That's what we were repeatedly being told. "Just wait and see." There is such a feeling of aloneness when you go through something like this. No one seems to understand just how devastating this can be to a family core. How could our family be falling apart and still have doctors telling us to "Just wait." I didn't want to wait.

My feelings were all over the place. I would range from feeling guilty because maybe I was making too much out of this when she would be better in a couple of weeks, to feeling very angry because no one seemed to notice that Libby wasn't getting better.

The couple of days had turned into weeks with very little change. Dave and I were going from the phase of being in shock, when you find out a loved one is injured to the time that things must be dealt with and taken care of. The shock of Libby's accident was wearing off. The new knowledge that we were now left with an almost helpless stranger, living in our home, was beginning to set in and so was anger.

CHAPTER 5

Progress

Kelly Cornish came to our home to tutor Libby in her school work. What I didn't know, when the school found Kelly and she agreed to tutor, was that she'd been Libby's student teacher in 6th grade, so they knew each other. The only information the school gave Kelly was that the reason she was being asked to tutor a student was medical and not because the student had been suspended for misbehaving. She was given directions to our home and told to come to our house after lunch every day. Kelly wasn't even given Libby's name until I called and told her. This wasn't because the school didn't care; this is because of the HIPAA (Health Insurance Portability and Accountability Act) laws in New York State and deal with privacy issues that we, as parents, tend to forget about.

When I spoke with Kelly on the phone, I gave her a little more detail. I explained that Libby had a concussion and was having difficulty with her memory and in fact had forgotten Math and Spanish entirely.

The first day Kelly came, she walked in and said "Hi Elizabeth, how have you been?"

Libby looked at Kelly, tentatively and just said "Hi."

"Remember me? I was your student teacher in 6th grade. When the school asked me to tutor someone, I was nervous at first and then I found out it was you. I was glad because you and I had a lot of fun together."

Libby looked at Kelly for a moment and then gave me that all too familiar *Here's another face I don't know* look.

I glanced at this woman standing in our living room, saw the confusion on her face and jumped in like a broken record. "Libby has a lot of memory loss from her accident and doesn't remember a lot of people yet." I'm amazed at how people actually seem to get their feelings hurt when Libby would admit that she didn't remember them. So I found myself in the middle, not only soothing my daughter, but the people standing in front of her with that shocked, hurt look on their faces. Kelly wasn't the first to have that look and definitely wasn't the last.

Kelly recovered quickly, sat down next to Libby and began pulling out books. In a calm voice and with, a smile on her face said. "Well, that's OK; we'll just get to know each other again then."

Kelly had a very quiet soothing voice, was extremely patient and interested in what she could do to help Libby learn. This way of teaching was good for Libby because realistically my daughter couldn't open a text book and find an answer to a question if you gave her the page it was on. Actually, she couldn't find the answer if she was given the paragraph it was in. She didn't know a lick of Algebra, even though she'd taken it in 8th grade and got high grades in it. She didn't know Spanish, even though once again she'd taken Spanish 1 in 8th grade and again got nineties in that subject.

She had a constant pressure headache that if asked on a scale of 1-10 with 10 being unbearable, Libby would just shrug and say, "Oh, it's not too bad it's only a 7 today."

Her stamina was about twenty minutes. After that, she had to stop and just be quiet for a while. If Kelly pushed her past those twenty minutes, she'd end up in tears, with a final outburst of, "I don't care! I don't even know what you're saying!"

If she had a few minutes to gather herself, sometimes she could push on a little more. On any given day Kelly might find her tutoring would last those twenty minutes. She wouldn't be able to get Libby to even start on another subject.

Within Kelly's first week, she realized that Libby had the ability to learn, but not to switch subjects. One day they'd work on Biology and the next Global and the next English. Each tutoring session could last from twenty minutes on a bad day to one and a half hours if Libby had a really good day.

Also, within that first week, we began to see that some teachers were very compassionate and understanding, but a lot of the time, they were in the dark about Libby's condition. The people I spoke with, who were in authority, neglected to follow through and pass information on to teachers. I had to e-mail each of them and explain Libby's situation, giving details of what she was capable of and what she wasn't capable of.

Most of Libby's teachers simply said, "Do what she can and we'll catch up when she's feeling better." I explained as much as I could to the nurse, the principal, and all the teachers, letting them know that we had no idea how long it would take for Libby to recover.

On October 19, Libby had her first appointment with the neurologist, Dr. Jenkins. The doctor performed some simple memory tests, asking Libby to draw a clock and a few other things. Most of the session was questions and answers. Once the doctor realized the extent of Libby's impairments, she ordered an MRI. She suggested that we meet with a clinical psychologist to have Libby tested and evaluated on just how big her deficits in learning were. She referred us to Dr. Rogers and once again assured us that given time, Libby should fully recover.

The MRI came back clean showing no brain bleeds, which confused me as much as comforted me. How could a test come back clean when someone couldn't remember her daily routine, had amnesia about a good portion of their life, lost about half her vocabulary and didn't seem to be improving? I naively thought that if she was hurt, it would just show up. The doctor assured us that this was a good thing and again said that Libby should fully recover.

We met with Dr. Rogers October 31 and got our first taste of sitting on "the couch" and talking. Libby clung to my arm and blocked out the entire appointment, while the doctor and I discussed her impairments.

I hated talking about Libby like she wasn't in the room, but she just wouldn't participate in any conversation at any of her doctors. It didn't matter that before each appointment, I'd say to Libby, "Honey, only you know how you feel. You have to be the one to tell the doctors. I can only tell them what I think you feel." Libby would agree, but then curl up and refuse to talk, once we got into the office.

As the doctor and I talked and Libby sat staring out the window, we discussed her prognosis. He stated that he didn't feel she should be tested at this point because, once Libby began to recover, the test results wouldn't be accurate. The testing itself was very extensive, lasting an entire day. He felt putting Libby through eight hours of testing was useless because at this point Libby wouldn't be able to tolerate it physically or mentally.

Dr. Rogers explained the way the brain recovers, telling us how the first six months, it's a rapid, almost daily recovery, but once she reached the six months' mark, progress then slows down. After a year it slows even more. He did say he'd like to test her six months post injury. That shook me. Six months? This was the first time I'd had any professional put a date to anything, besides give it a few days or another week.

I finally got the nerve to ask. "Dr. Rogers, how long is it going to take Libby to recover?"

He didn't sugar coat it, but laid it on the line and simply said "A minimum of three to six months. Usually once the swelling recedes, the brain recovers rapidly, but in some cases like Elizabeth's, it just takes longer. After six months, the recovery slows down and after the first year, it's an even slower recovery."

Dr. Rogers paused and then said. "You do have a lawyer, don't you?"

A lawyer? No way! I was angry at the school for what had happened to Libby, but we hadn't even considered a lawyer. Up until now, we had everyone telling us give to it a week or two. I'd been clinging to that promise of a speedy recovery, and hadn't really let myself think yet about the long term prognosis.

"No, we don't. Do you really think we need one?"

"I suggest you find one. Mrs. Parker, this injury your daughter sustained isn't just going to go away. This could take months for her to even find a semblance of what her normal used to be. You may find that she may need to make a new normal." Dr. Rogers watched me intently and saw the shock register on my face.

"Mrs. Parker, you may actually find that Elizabeth may not even want to do the same things she used to do. They may be too hard for her now, and she may find new things to take their place. This is a very transitional time for her. You need to be aware of this. I honestly can't tell you how long this is going to take and what Elizabeth's outcome will be, only time will tell us that, but I can tell you, she isn't just going to wake up and be better."

"Dr. Rogers her X-rays, CAT scan and MRI were all clean, how can this take that long if it doesn't even show up on the tests?" My mind was having a very hard time absorbing what this man was telling me. My daughter had to find a new normal? What did that mean?

"Well, fifteen percent of traumatic brain injuries don't show up on conventional tests, the most accurate testing at this point is the neuropsychological testing that we'll do at six months, if she still has deficits at that point. In the meantime I'd like to keep up on her progress. I'd like to schedule appointments once a month to determine how much progress Elizabeth is making, and in the meantime, yes, I think you better find a lawyer."

Libby and I left Dr. Rogers's office and I honestly think I was in shock. I couldn't think. I had no idea what to tell Dave when we got home or the school and now we had to look for a lawyer. I had no idea where to start looking. In the past, we'd only used lawyers for our real estate purchases. We'd never been involved in a lawsuit, never had to hire an attorney to get our boys out of hot water. We were true country bumpkins, when it came to legal matters.

After Dave and I discussed what to do, we decided to start with lawyers who were out of town because we were considering suing a school system. We didn't want any personal ties. I wasn't even sure if our local lawyers had ever handled a case where a school system was sued. It didn't set well with us. We were both raised to handle things responsibly and if you messed up, you paid for it. If someone else messed up, you worked it out with them. I think, because the school administration had treated this from the beginning like it had never happened, that fact alone let us pick up the phone and start searching.

Neither Dave nor I had ever attended Libby's school, but my parents both had, my younger sisters had, my sons had and I felt a personal tie. How do we sue a place where you knew some of the teachers personally? We decided to just call and find out what our options were, just because the doctor had been quite adamant about finding an attorney.

I called a couple offices in some of the bigger towns near us, left messages with them explaining our situation, and never even got to speak with an attorney that first day. I waited several days for someone to call me back, which never happened, so on the next attempt, I branched out. I found yellow pages from our nearest big city, picked the biggest ad I could find and dialed the number. Wow, the receptionist transferred me to an actual attorney. I spoke with Frank Walker for the first time and explained our situation. He seemed very pleasant and explained the laws to me, telling me that an injury had to last at least ninety days to qualify as an actual injury. I explained that Dr. Rogers stated her recovery would be from three to six months. Frank agreed to meet with us the following week.

That began a three year relationship with the Walker Law Firm. What we initially did was file papers with the intent to sue, since that had to be done before ninety days post accident. Then we would wait to see how Libby recovered before we actually decided to pursue anything further. Secretly, I was hoping that if the school realized they might be sued over this, just maybe they'd begin treating Libby's accident and her deficits a little more seriously.

It was the first of November, five weeks since the accident. Her deficits were pretty much the same as when she'd started back to school, but Dave and I were now being told that school policies prevented them from treating Libby any differently than any other child in their class. I was now being repeatedly told that they couldn't do anything unless we had Libby tested and she was classified as learning disabled. At the same time I had her neuropsychologist telling us that it was useless to test her now, but to wait another five months. When I mentioned this to the school, they would tell me they were sorry, but it was out of their hands.

I asked almost daily, "Isn't there something you can do until Libby improves?"

A few of the teachers were becoming insistent that Libby keep up. I really can't blame them. They didn't have any information on Libby's recovery unless I told them directly. I tried to keep each teacher caught up with Libby's abilities weekly via e-mail.

We had also reached that point in a normal concussion where the injured person usually is recovered enough to get on with life. It was at this time that I began to hear the murmurings of, "It's just a concussion." I'm sure at some point in their teaching careers all the teachers had an athlete in their classroom that had got their bell rung and for a couple of weeks they knew that he would be out of commission, but then that student recovered and things went back to normal. Libby was different.

Her biology teacher surprised me the most. Here was the woman my daughter insisted on going to see the day after her accident who told her not to worry about a thing, but just get better. This woman had now turned into a cold, seemingly uncaring teacher who simply refused to give an inch. She was insistent that we must follow all state regulations to the letter, but when I asked her for a detailed description of those regulations I would only get evasive answers.

Kelly started doing Biology labs at home with Libby, the simple ones that we had supplies for on hand, only to find out that Mrs. Floorz was now refusing to give Libby credit for lab hours. Apparently in New York State, a student must complete so many lab hours to even be allowed to take the Regents exam at the end of the year. She was letting Libby do the labs, spending hours trying to catch up with the rest of the class, and then not giving her credit for the hours it took to complete the lab, because she wasn't actually witnessing the work being done. It didn't seem to matter to her that Kelly kept track of the hours.

Kelly e-mailed each of the teachers and explained Libby's condition, telling them all that at this point in Libby's recovery, she learned best by having someone read the information to her. Once Mrs. Floorz got the e-mail, she refused to send chapter tests home because "it wouldn't be fair to the other students."

Her explanation was, "I don't read out loud to them, or leave the book open for them, so you can't for Elizabeth."

When we tried to explain that an open book meant nothing because Libby couldn't read from it, it didn't matter. She informed Kelly that she had permission from the superintendent to withhold tests until further notice. We tried explaining to Mrs. Floorz through e-mails and conversations that Libby wasn't even capable of picking an answer out of the book. We'd tried during homework assignments. Even if we pointed out the paragraph that the answer was in, she couldn't find it. We were just hoping that pictures on the page would possibly remind her of what she had studied.

To me it was simple. Libby needed someone to read out loud and help her find answers in books. She could learn and remember at least a portion, if this was followed. Without Kelly's assistance, Libby was lost. So shouldn't a school be able to just help that student learn by the best teaching method for that student? I thought so.

Kelly tried getting in touch with Mrs. Crabner, our superintendent, but was told every time that she was busy and would call her back. (She never did.) I went to the principal about what this was doing to Libby's grades. If she wasn't allowed to take the tests, she couldn't get a grade. Mr. King actually suggested pulling Libby from Biology, just to make it easier.

"On whom," I asked? I could feel anger building, "Libby or Mrs. Floorz? Libby's doing the work, but if Mrs. Floorz won't send tests home, how does she expect her to remember what she's studied once this is finally resolved? She doesn't even accept Kelly as a legitimate tutor, so where is this getting us? When you hired Kelly she must have had the proper credentials, right?"

Mr. King agreed that she did indeed have all the necessary credentials.

"Then why are you allowing this?"

"Mrs. Parker, I think possibly the best solution to this issue would be to pull Libby from Biology and let her take it again next year. This would give her an extra study hall, if she needs it. Possibly, we should consider pulling her from a couple core classes, just to make it easier for Libby."

"I don't want her pulled from any classes yet. I want Libby to have the opportunity to try to pass and if she can't, then so be it, but you can't take the opportunity away. She just needs some help right now until she recovers." I knew Libby's determination to get good grades. If she knew what was now being suggested it would crush her.

I was upset, so in a calm demeanor, Mr. King said he'd see what he could do. Give him a little time and he'd get with the school administration and then get back with me. I left our first real parent/principal meeting feeling like nothing had been accomplished. I had no answers, or even a clue how to resolve this issue.

The next day, when Kelly came, we discussed again what to do with Biology and Kelly was visibly upset. "If I'm not a qualified teacher, then what am I doing here?" She asked. "I can't believe she's doing this. I didn't think a teacher had the right to withhold a subject. I think it's against Libby's civil rights or something."

Here I am, a Mom who wants to screamat the entire school. "Look what you did to my daughter!" Instead I pleaded with principals, e-mailed and tried to reason with Biology teachers, believed every word that the school was telling me because, after all, *they* are the authority figures. I was raised to respect those in authority, but in my heart I knew what was happening here just wasn't right.

I had a daughter who couldn't keep up with what was expected of her. She was just entering her Regents classes and had some tough classes to keep up with. Libby had started the year out with high expectations and in just a few short weeks it had all fallen apart. Now we were at the end of the first marking period. I had some teachers still being very patient, others starting to question when Libby was coming back to class. Others were digging their heels in and refusing to cooperate at all. There had to be a better way than all this scrambling around e-mailing each teacher, trying to reason with some. Speaking up and saying "That's just not possible yet, or we'll give it a try." All the while feeling like we were on a sinking ship and we didn't even have a captain.

On our next visit to Dr. Rogers, I explained what the school situation was and his reasoning was.

"Hmmmm, they expect Libby to perform like the other students and there are no exceptions? Well, then, I suggest we tell those teachers that we'll just have to walk into the class room, clip every student in the head so then it is even. We can't make this go away just to suit them."

Of course he was being sarcastic, but it was a thought I'd often had while being told they couldn't treat Libby special. In reality, what he did was write a letter to the school. Dr. Rogers suggested introducing one period at a time to integrate Libby back into her old schedule.

Two weeks went by while I waited for Mr. King to get our Biology problem straightened out. When we got Dr. Rogers's letter I immediately contacted the school and set up a general conference with all of Libby's teachers. Dave, Kelly and I showed up at the school knowing that, though it was a general meeting, our biggest issue was going to be Biology.

After nervously sitting in chairs positioned outside the door watching each teacher file in, we were finally called in and sat round-table fashion with Mr. King sitting directly across from us. He began speaking and asked that each teacher take a moment to tell us how they felt that Libby was doing.

Each teacher took a turn asking questions, or explaining their concerns, a few just giving us encouragement. Mr. Martinez (Spanish) simply said he was willing to wait until "I can see her lights on," before he asked anything of her. What an appropriate statement. So often, Libby walked around with this blank stare, but when she understood something, we could see that old twinkle come into her eyes. Mrs. Higgins (English) told us how much she missed Libby, asked when she'd be back and stated that she was willing to wait for back assignments too.

Mr. King brought up the subject, asking about pulling Libby from some of her core classes just to make it easier on her. I pulled Dr. Rogers' letter out of my folder and handed it to him. He read the letter through, and then read it aloud for everyone, when I asked him to. I felt that the letter explained all the issues clearly.

Thank you for your referral of Elizabeth Parker. I met with her and her mother for an initial interview on 10/31/06. As you know, she experienced a concussion on 9/25/06 when her school bus was struck from behind. She has subsequently had multiple cognitive difficulties, headaches, pain, fatigue, and problems doing school work. In discussing the situation in detail with Elizabeth and her mother, it was clear that Elizabeth is experiencing rapid changes, although continues to have significant impairments in her ability to do school work. Since Elizabeth is in a period of dynamic recovery, I question how useful a neuropsychological evaluation will be at this time. Any information and insight gained is likely to become quickly outdated, making the effort and expense without much purpose.

What is more important at this stage is for Elizabeth's teachers, tutor and family to be sensitive to her fluctuating capacity. She should be encouraged to do more when she is able to focus adequately on the material presented. Elizabeth appears reasonably motivated. It is important for people working with her to understand that she will reach a point when she is overloaded, where her brain just shuts down. If she is pushed at that point, it will be frustrating for everyone and she is likely to become emotional. When it gets to that point, a point which should not be too hard to recognize, Elizabeth needs to rest preferable taking a nap. The length of the nap will depend on the degree of her fatigue. If she is in school, she may need to go to the nurse's station and skip a class, or part of a class.

It is also important to understand that Elizabeth's recall memory will take longer to recover than her recognition memory. Therefore, I expect her to do poorly with tests that are not multiple choices. As a result, at the present time, it would be better for her to be tested using multiple choice tests. Since her status is changing dynamically, she should periodically be probed using more challenging standards. As her tolerance improves, she should be able to return to school full time with on-demand access to the nurse's station. I feel there is no need to remove Elizabeth from any core classes at this time, due to the rate of her recovery. She should, with these accommodations be successful in her classes. Elizabeth appears motivated to return to her normal school routine and I do not see any secondary gain issues being present. Testing will be considered when she is six months post injury.

Then it was Mrs. Floorz' turn. She immediately stated how she was also compassionate to Libby's needs. I heard Dave snort in disbelief, and quickly placed my hand on his thigh under the table, while she continued speaking. Her main concern was Libby's ability to meet the criteria for Biology in NY.

"Libby's not meeting the criteria because you're not giving her credit for her lab hours that she does with Kelly and you refuse to send home chapter tests." I stated firmly my anger already starting to build.

"I have permission from the superintendent to withhold those tests, and if I can't see Elizabeth actually doing labs, how do I know how many hours she's worked on them?" Mrs. Floorz responded, her face turning a bright crimson.

"Because you have an employee of the school monitoring her hours," I said hotly!

"Mrs. Floorz, I have all the required credits to teach. What makes you think I'm not qualified to write on a piece of paper how long it took Libby to complete a lab? That's insulting. And it's insulting that you don't think I'm competent to administer a chapter test. I've been hired by this very school in the past to monitor Regents' finals. I think what your doing is against Libby's civil rights. You are not allowed, according to state law to refuse to teach a subject to any student." Kelly leaned forward in her seat as she responded to Mrs. Floorz, as did every other teacher in the room.

Mr. King intervened. "Hold on here. I think before this situation gets out of hand, we need to have a private meeting with this teacher. We can discuss this later at a more appropriate time. I'll take our conversation to the proper administration and then I'll be able to get back to you with a solution."

Though he was trying to let us know that this should be a private conversation, I glanced around and noticed that every teacher was watching Mrs. Floorz with great interest. I got the distinct impression that some were enjoying what was happening. I felt just a little obligated to those teachers who'd been supportive, along with the fact that the last time I heard Mr. King tell me that, I still was waiting for an answer. I couldn't stop myself.

"No I'm sorry I don't accept that solution," I said, staring directly at Mr. King. "If you recall, I was in your office two weeks ago, begging for your help. You said to me "You make a very valid point, Mrs. Parker; I'll get with administration and get back to you with an answer." So I'm sure you'll understand why I don't want to accept your suggestion now. I don't plan on waiting another two weeks. This matter needs to be resolved now."

At that point, my husband, who'd remained silent, turned to Mrs. Floorz and said. "I'd just like to ask you one question? What gives you the right to tell us what our child's needs are? You've done nothing but tell us what we can't do. You've made no suggestions on how to resolve this. What makes you better than her family physician, a neurologist and a neuropsychologist, when they're telling the school Libby needs certain accommodations right now and you won't even listen to their suggestions?"

"I'm just following state regulations," Mrs. Floorz said, now near tears.

"You show me the regulations that say you have to be standing over her monitoring her lab hours and where you can rightfully withhold tests! My wife has asked you repeatedly for a list of those regulations you keep throwing in our face and as of yet, we haven't seen any."

I placed my hand on Dave's arm trying to let him know he'd gone far enough. When Dad gets mad, everyone in the house knows. It has served its purpose keeping two teenage boys in line and has done well when he feels his children aren't being treated fairly, but once on a roll, I have to admit, Dave can get pretty hot under the collar and say things that might be considered inappropriate.

"Look Mr. and Mrs. Parker this is not the time or place to air our differences," Mr. King stated firmly trying to regain some control.

"This is exactly the time and place," Dave responded still fuming. "My wife has been trying to resolve this nicely for a month and has gotten nowhere. I want an answer now."

"Well, would you be willing to compromise," Mr. King asked?

"I think we're the only ones who have been compromising," Dave retorted. His voice had gone down several decibels though and I removed my hand from his arm.

"If Mrs. Floorz agrees to send home the chapter tests for Mrs. Cornish to administer, would you be willing to bring Libby in once in a while to make up labs? Most of the labs you can't do at home anyway and this way Mrs. Floorz can monitor Libby's progress and she'll get credit for lab hours."

"I would agree to that as long as you understand we'd have to play it by ear," I said looking at Mr. King. "Libby has good days and bad days. On her bad days, even Kelly has to leave early. I'd be willing to bring her down on her good days after school, but that will cut into Kelly's tutoring time. You need to understand that." I glanced at Kelly and then at the teachers in the room. "You all need to understand that this is going to change things for her other classes because Kelly sometimes stays past 2:30, if Libby is on a roll with one of your assignments."

Every teacher nodded in understanding. I'm not really sure if they cared for the arrangement, but I know one thing, they certainly didn't want to stir up any more controversy. So an agreement was reached and we left our first general teacher/parent meeting feeling like we'd finally accomplished something.

For us, this was a big deal. It was the first time we'd actually felt like we had control of something again. Everything else was out of our control, as we walked around on eggshells trying not to upset Libby, explaining and explaining again to the people around us what was going on with our daughter.

For over a month, Dave and I felt like everything in the world was circling around us and we just couldn't grab hold and slow things down. We ran to doctor appointments. I ran every morning to pick Libby up from school. We ran for orchestra, and lessons and school meetings. I waited every morning by the phone, afraid if I left the house, Libby would need me. Our family dynamics had changed drastically. Everything seemed so out of control for us that it felt really good just to stand there and finally feel like we had just a little control over our lives again.

In the past, whenever I mentioned this incident at our school, common reaction has been "But schools can't do that kind of thing." or "What about the *No Child Left Behind* Act? I thought this sort of thing didn't happen anymore." We were naïve. We'd never had to deal with special accommodations before for any of our children and didn't have a clue how to resolve issues within a school district. The process is frustrating because so often parents don't know where to turn or who to ask the right questions to.

I'm sure this particular Biology teacher thought she was doing the right thing. She was sure that Libby had missed too much of her class to ever be able to pass this course. But her lack of empathy to our situation drove a big wedge between this teacher and not only me, but Libby, for the remainder of the year.

In our situation, we were finding that our school sorely lacked communication between school and family. We'd had to fight for a tutor, spend endless hours communicating with each teacher individually, and beg our principal to understand Libby's needs. We felt very alone.

I now know there are organizations out there to help parents, so they don't have to fight alone. I understand now that only a few school districts willingly jump in and find solutions, without one of these organizations backing the parent, showing them how to maneuver through the system. The red tape is unbelievable. As a parent with a child who now had a disability, I was clueless. Little by little, though, we made progress and learned with each mistake.

CHAPTER 6

Ups and Downs

Everything about our life was changing. Dave and I had no idea what to do or who to listen to. Doctors told us wait a few weeks, and then a few months when in reality, only the injured brain can tell when it's ready to heal. It really is a "wait and see" game. In the meantime, we grasped at any little hope or sign of recovery. It was discouraging, moving from that place of hoping and praying things would be over soon, to that new territory of preparing for the future and the unknown.

Libby was changing too. While her brain tried to heal, she still had to deal with the right now. The only way Libby could do that was to establish a rigid routine. She was trying so hard to keep up with everything around her, learning that everything in her room had to have a home or she'd forget where she put it. She was trying to remember to write her assignments down, when she was at school, so she didn't forget her homework, trying to keep her stamina up getting up in the morning, coming home for lunch, Kelly in the afternoon, labs later in the afternoon, sometimes. This was her new world and any deviation from this daily routine could throw her into an emotional storm.

What is an emotional storm you ask? An emotional storm is quite a sight to behold. It is a combination of exhaustion, TBI (Traumatic Brain Injury) vulnerability, being a teenager with all the respective hormones raging away, PTSD, (Post Traumatic Stress Disorder) and TBI fatigue all thrown into one moment. The brain ceases to function properly, shuts down and leaves the person totally unable to perform at all. The brain basically tells the body to stop doing what it's doing, which leaves a bunch of overwhelming emotions raging, inside the person, full force. Because the brain has now shut down, it's incapable of telling its body how to deal with those emotions, leaving the body virtually defenseless.

An emotional storm starts small, usually with Libby quietly stating, "My head hurts."

If I didn't catch on right away, and said something like, "Ok, let's finish this last question in your homework."

A veiled look would come over her eyes, tears would well up, but she might not say a word. I, at this point, have now realized she's done, but it's too late, because I haven't learned that quiet is the only solution, so instead I say, "Put your books away, you can be done for now."

That's all it takes. One more command, simple as it may be, "Put your books away," is impossible to her because her brain has now shut down. All she hears is noise. I have now learned to take her by the hand or arm, lead her to her bed and simply say, "Lie down."

In the beginning we didn't understand what an emotional storm was, so Dave and I would try to tell her to go to her room, once she'd reached that point where she began crying and screaming at us in nonsense sentences. We simply did not understand that she really couldn't. Her brain had switched to survival mode and was only capable of telling her body to perform its basic functions. The tears would turn to sobbing; she would literally fall to the floor and lie there. No amount of talking, coaxing or yelling could get her up. It was heart wrenching, watching this "used to be bubbly, smiling girl" lying on the floor in a heap sobbing her heart out. Eventually, sometimes a couple of minutes and sometimes a half hour later, she would pull herself up and go to her bed, falling into a deep sleep for at least six hours.

Dr. Rogers explained to us that she has no control at this point. The only thing we can do is distance ourselves until it runs its course. As long as she was safe, just leave her be. The problem was, if I walked away, her sobbing and screaming would be louder and last longer, because now her safety net (me) was gone too. I was torn between leaving for my own peace of mind and staying where Libby could see me, knowing that if I did stay the storm might end sooner.

These storms happened at home, most of the time, because home was where she felt safe. Home was her safety zone, where she didn't always have to keep that stiff upper lip and she could just let loose. Occasionally, she would loose control at school and I'd get a call to come get her. Nobody knew what to do with Libby, when she had these emotional meltdowns.

I now know, after three years of study, and experience with TBI, emotional storms are very common and usually dealt with at a hospital or in rehabilitation center, once a TBI patient comes out of his or her coma. We had to learn to deal with it at home with no one helping us, except our once a month visit to Dr. Rogers. TBI patients who are released from the hospital with a diagnosis of post concussive syndrome are given basically no warnings or advice and their families are left to deal with what comes along.

When Libby's meltdowns started, I ran to our public library and took out every book I could find on TBI, looking for answers. What I found was that most of the books I read were about people who had suffered severe brain injuries and the books talked about rehabilitation. There might be a paragraph or two on mild TBI, but that was it. There were no answers ready for me that I could find. Libby wasn't in a hospital with professional staff around twenty fours hours a day, she was home. There was no manual that told us how to deal with what we were going through, so we just muddled along.

Patience was now the new "normal" for Dave and me. Every word we spoke or action we took with Libby, we had to think differently about. Every emotion we felt, we tried to hide, because if we were upset, Libby would be in tears thinking she had done something wrong.

"This is new to her too," I kept telling myself. "If it's this bad for me, what must it feel like inside Libby's head?" When these thoughts raced through my head, I began to feel guilty for feeling them. This was Libby's injury not mine. She was the one going through all the memory loss. All I had to do was watch.

Brain Injury doesn't just happen to the one person. It happens to the entire family. It took me years to learn that, so I dealt with the guilt, along with a whole range of emotions. Fear, I felt fear for the unknown. What will my daughter be like years from now? Will we have to care for her the rest of her life? Will she ever be able to control her emotions again? Will she ever be able to remember? I knew if we had to care for Libby for the rest of her life, we could and would without hesitation, but still I was afraid for her.

Everything we did was trial and error. If we found something that worked we stuck to it. If it didn't work, we'd shake our heads, tell ourselves, "Well, we won't do that again," and move on. The frustration was unbelievable for all of us. I was starting to get doubts that our lives would ever resemble the lives we used to have. The worst was seeing Libby's face, that face, that used to be so happy and smiling, now filled with scowls and tears. She was afraid to go anywhere by herself or do anything beyond what her brain would tell her she could do in that moment. She didn't seem capable of thinking about tomorrow, only right now.

We eventually learned the warning signs of an emotional storm and Dr. Rogers helped us with strategies to stop a storm before it started. If her emotions started to rise, anyone in the house was allowed to signal a time out. We agreed it would be the football signal of making a T with our hands. Once a time out was called, we all went to separate areas of the house for quiet. If Dave and I went together, Libby felt we could still talk about what was happening. That wasn't fair to her, so we each picked a spot in the house. Libby's spot was her room, mine was the office and Dave went to the bedroom. After Libby felt she'd regained control and allowed her brain just to rest and bring down the emotional level to tolerable, we could try to continue doing what we were doing. If Libby's emotions again went up, we called it a day.

We were so lost. We didn't know how to be parents anymore. All the old things we relied on went out the window, replaced with the unknown. We had doctors telling us to be patient and wait and see. We had a school trying to be patient, but still following their policies not treating Libby different than any other student. But she was, and all our requests and Dr. Rogers suggestions were ignored. How could we mend our family, when it seemed the outside world either didn't understand or just didn't care?

As parents we now had this teenage stranger living with us. We didn't know how to respond to Libby. Here was someone with big gaps in her memory, watching people come up to her and talk, knowing she should know them, but just didn't. Once her memory started coming back, it wasn't like in the movies where the patient gets another bump on the head and all of a sudden they remember, or suddenly something in their past flashes through their brain and the memories just flood back. Her recovery was disjointed and confusing and made no sense.

When Libby began to remember, even that wasn't what we expected. In the movies the injured person suddenly has a flash back and taa-daa, presto chango, she's better. Oh, so not true in the real world.

Libby was sitting with me on the sofa doing Biology homework one evening. She was just starting to remember how to read and write again. We went over an answer to a chapter review question. She began writing her answer so I looked down to read it and it didn't make sense to me. No words that I could understand. I stopped her.

"Honey, what are you writing," I questioned?

"Why?" she asked then looked down at her paper, paused a second and began frowning.

"I didn't write that!"

"Yea, you did, but I can't understand it." I was watching her face trying to figure out what was going on. Suddenly in a rare moment, Libby began to smile.

"Oh," she giggled. "It's Spanish."

"Well, what does it say?"

"I don't know, I can't read it" she said beaming, "but I know it's Spanish."

That was the end of homework for the night, because at that point, not only could she not read back the Spanish she'd written, but she couldn't write in English either. When she tried, the smile was replaced once again with a scowl. Her brain had thrown in a crossed signal between the two languages for just a moment, like a glitch in a computer program and it had shut down her ability to do either.

Another day, we were working on an English assignment and I noticed that Libby kept looking at her algebra book. I couldn't keep her focused, so finally I gave up and asked her what she was thinking. She picked the Algebra book up and said. "I think I can do this. What page am I on?"

She began leafing through the pages. I looked through her assignment sheet and gave her a page number and she found the page quickly which in itself was a huge step because she hadn't been able to do that before. She picked up a paper, folded it in half the long way, like she used to do before her accident, and wrote down the first problem.

Up until this point, numbers had been beyond Libby's ability. She'd lost everything she'd learned about algebra, didn't even recall that she'd taken a year of it already and got pretty decent grades in it. We'd been avoiding Math so far, because the problems were beyond Libby's ability. So, to have her pick up her book and start working problems and write an entire page full of answers, before she raised her head and looked at me, was remarkable.

"I remember," was all she said.

I was thrilled. I wanted to jump around the room and hoot and holler and sing, but instead I just hugged her and said, "Good job, Libby."

The next day, when Kelly came, I told her that Libby remembered how to do algebra again. Kelly immediately got out the book and sat down with her, hoping to catch up on some assignments. That all too familiar look was coming over Libby's face. Something was wrong.

What's wrong?" I asked.

"My head hurts," she said, resting her head on her folded arms on the table.

Kelly and I were becoming much attuned to Libby and knew that, even though last night had been a huge leap forward, today was another day. Kelly opened the book and asked Libby if she wanted to try. Libby looked at the book for a few minutes; asked for the page number. She began flipping through pages until she got to the end of the book, closed the book, looked at Kelly and said with no emotion at all.

"I can't find it."

And there we were. Back to square one. She couldn't find the page and couldn't do algebra. For one brief hour, it had come back to her and then was gone. Or so we thought. The following week we got her grade back on the assignment she'd done and it was a forty five. Apparently Libby had the concept, but had transposed numbers in almost half the problems.

We were starting to get brief glimmers of recovery and then it would be gone, who knows for how long? Because of her amnesia, when Libby started back to school, it was like starting in a new school, not knowing anyone. Little by little she relearned or remembered where her classes were and gradually, one friend at a time Libby began to remember most of them. I would catch her looking through her yearbook, when she got home from school, trying to put everything back in place in her memory. One particular day she pointed out a boy, where through the years, some days they were good friends other days they were fighting. She pointed to his picture in the yearbook. "In first grade when I had real long hair I think he used to pull it. Do I like him or don't I?"

I laughed. "Yes to both, Libby. Through all your school years you've never been able to make up your mind."

"That's because he picks on me so much," she said, smiling at the picture.

She pointed to the picture of a girl next to the boy. "I know I don't like her. She's always been mean." Then Libby got this little, mysterious smile on her face and she looked up at me. It was that old impish grin I used to see all the time. "I remembered her a while ago. She's been coming up to me almost every day, asking me 'Do you remember me yet?' and I keep telling her, 'Nope'. I really do, but I'm not going to tell her that because I know it bugs her that I don't remember her."

Both Libby and I laughed. I realized that my daughter was starting to think deeper than basic memories. Her sense of humor was starting to show a little again, twisted yes, but still humor.

"Honey, that's not nice," I said, though I couldn't quite wipe the smile from my face. "You have to tell her you remember her."

"Yea, I know. I will," she said still smiling. I'm not sure if she ever did.

It became a contest at the school who Libby would remember next. Her friends took it as a symbol of where she ranked their friendship, but in reality, it was something that was said, or who was standing in front of her at the moment her brain was ready to receive more information. I realized this when Libby took almost a month to remember one of her very best friends, Claire. Libby and Claire had been inseparable in junior high, spending nights at each others houses, baking Christmas cookies together and decorating them. Claire had almost become that appendage that was considered family. She went to family dinners with us and got along great with Kiara, Libby's cousin.

Libby's memory came back in stages. A little here and then a step backwards, but gradually, her memory of certain things would begin to stay a little longer before she'd go backward again. About ten weeks after her accident, Kelly and I noticed that her reading was starting to come back. She could actually understand a sentence, though certain words would stop her dead in her tracks.

We were working on a history assignment. Libby was slowly reading to me when she came upon the word *invade*. She asked me what the word was and I pronounced it for her. Libby shook her head no.

"No, that's not it Mom, it looks like *in- vah- day*."

"Nope, it's invade." I pronounced the word correctly again, but once again she shook her head no. And that was the end of reading for the day. We couldn't move past the word. We found that the simple words were coming back, but in reality, I think she had to relearn most of the complex words, which took time. While she relearned these words, often times her Spanish knowledge, which had been locked away, would surface. Rather than pronounce a word with English intonations, she would interject Spanish pronunciations. There was progress, but to weed through the cross firings her brain would, send was exhausting. Often, after a day or two of progress, we'd notice that Libby would crash, both physically and mentally. When she crashed, she'd be bedridden, sound asleep, sometimes for a full twenty four hours, missing school and tutoring.

She still stuttered when she spoke, often searching for simple words to complete a sentence. I'd try to jump in, with what I thought the right word might be, not realizing that her brain just wasn't ready to retrieve that lost word yet. Most of the time she'd just shake her head no and give up trying to talk. Other times, she just couldn't let go until she'd figured it out, often ending in tears.

In time, we began measuring her progress, not in little moments, but in days. Today was a good day. She could read, write, do a little math, and remember one word of Spanish, smile. Today was a bad day, meltdowns, migraines, sleeping for six hours during the day and arguing over absolutely everything.

With what seemed like a snails' pace, Libby slowly improved. Enough to give us glimmers of our old Libby and give us hope that whatever was going on in her head just might, in time go away. Just maybe the doctors were right.

We were working with her doctors, trying to find ways to diminish the emotional storms and Dr. Perry switched her Zoloft to Celexa, which seemed to help with her anxiety attacks, and not make her as groggy. She recommended a chiropractor for Libby's neck and back pain. We began taking her several times a week, hoping that if the pain was reduced, it'd be one less thing interfering with her concentration and recovery.

I hate to use the word "whiplash"; it's almost a dirty word that as soon as someone says it people think of that person in the courtroom with the neck brace on, faking it. Whiplash has a bad reputation. We found that when we mentioned Libby's whiplash, we usually got that "Oh, yea, right!" look from anyone but her doctors.

Dr. Jenkins prescribed Periactin for Libby's headaches which had by now been divided into two categories: Pressure headache and Migraine headache. We were waiting to see if this new "med" would help with the pain. One of the problems with her new prescription was it caused weight gain. Slowly, Libby's weight began creeping up higher and higher. She didn't seem to notice as we bought new clothes in larger sizes, but what could we do? She couldn't exercise yet, without being in horrible pain. Any increase in her heart rate would cause excruciating pressure headaches and we were being told that the meds were necessary to control her emotions and headaches.

We got a membership at the local YMCA and for several months Libby worked out on the machines there, or swam in their pool. We found that the machines even at minimum weight caused Libby more pain the next few days. To me, it seemed that when she exercised her brain threw in another crossed signal. Instead of that sore feeling you get the following day after exercise, Libby wouldn't be able to move her neck or back without being in excruciating pain. Her brain was telling her she was still injured.

We tried swimming in the pool when the exercise became too much. Libby had been an excellent swimmer before her accident so the first day in the pool I walked into the water with her and started swimming towards the other end only to find Libby wasn't with me. She was standing in the same spot with a look of total panic in her face. I swam back to her immediately.

"What's the matter?" I asked.

"I can't..." her eyes filled with tears.

"C'mon Libby it's warm you'll love this."

"I – I can't...I can't remember how."

I never gave it a thought that she might not remember how to swim. We spent the first day with Libby clinging to the edge of the pool in a panic. The second time she put her face in the water to see if she could remember how to hold her breath under water. Once she realized that she could do that, Libby finally got brave enough to let go of the edge and relax. By the third time, she was swimming again.

It's not an easy task to remember to try to live normally. People, even our close family, didn't understand. How do you live a normal life, going out to dinner, visiting friends or family, going swimming, when your daughter might not remember the people, place or how to swim? Just picking a food item off a menu became a difficult task because Libby would study and study the menu until I gave the warning. "Pick or I'll pick for you." That would usually lead to tears because she just couldn't decide. The everyday routine of school was still continuously looming over us too. My days were filled with waiting by the phone in the morning, hoping Libby could make it through the day. I didn't go anywhere, because I'd learned that, even if she left in a good mood that morning, one crisis at school could cause a meltdown.

I got a call from Libby, for it seemed the twentieth time that month, asking me to come get her. I always started my end of the conversation with asking her to try to hold out for just a little longer. I would wait for her response to see if this was just a minor crisis or "The big one". If I could talk her into staying a little longer, I felt like I'd accomplished a major feat. This time she burst into tears and just said, "No, come get me." All because she'd asked a question in Math and the teacher hadn't responded so Libby could understand. She then forgot where she was going, once she was in the hallway heading to her next class and had to ask a student. Once to that class, which she was late arriving at, she was informed by the teacher, after she continued to ask him to explain something repeatedly; that she was the neediest student he'd ever met. She held on through class but once it was over, she ran to the orchestra room and huddled in a corner of a practice room until Mr. Michaels found her.

Then, once a week, every Wednesday evening, we'd pile in the car, headache or not, tired or not and head to her violin lesson. Some days Libby seemed able to play just fine and other days she didn't seem to even be able to understand where her fingers belonged on the strings, but she was determined to go. Every Sunday we'd head for orchestra practice and she'd spend three hours there. I questioned Libby asking her if this wasn't just too much, but she adamantly protested any suggestion of giving up her music for a while. Occasionally, her headaches would be bad enough; we'd have to leave practice early. Practicing exhausted Libby and hurt her neck and back, but she wouldn't give up. Music was what kept her going. It didn't matter how hard it was. It was something she could do and was good at and if she had to sleep when she got home, it didn't matter to her.

Every weekday morning, Libby would get up, get ready for school and get on that bus ready to try again. I can't explain the mixed emotions I felt watching her walk down the drive to get on the bus after a horrible day at school the day before. My heart would ache, while I stood at the door praying that "today will be a better day" so filled with pride just because she didn't pull the covers over her head and simply give up.

Once home, I'd give Libby lunch which sometimes she ate and other times she just pushed away in exhaustion and went to lie down on the sofa until Kelly arrived. Kelly would show up around 12:30 p.m. and would feel her way around Libby's abilities for the day. Some days, they'd accomplish an entire week of English assignments, and other days they might get through half of a global studies assignment. Then, if it was a good day, we'd be off to school again for an hour of lab assignments. More times than not, Libby didn't understand the lab, or the way Mrs. Floorz tried to explain an assignment.

I was beginning to notice that Libby would insist that a teacher explain if she didn't understand. "Wait! Say that again, I don't get it," became an often used phrase while doing labs.

We found also that Libby couldn't see into a microscope. She would look and just not be able to see what was on the slide. Every time she tried, she got a blinding headache from the bright backlight. It seemed that Biology was going to be her downfall. I sat with Libby during labs and became her lab partner. I helped her measure, did the looking into the microscope while Libby wrote our findings down. Mrs. Floorz sat at her desk and graded papers.

Sometimes the teacher would offer to help Libby with particular assignments, but she had a very hard time explaining in ways that Libby could understand. Mrs. Floorz would just repeat the same thing over and over, never changing words around that might help Libby understand. Once she saw tears in Libby's eyes, she would give up and just let me take over. Occasionally, I would receive e-mails from Mrs. Floorz telling me that she just didn't think Libby would pass this course; that there were just too many obstacles in her way.

I would always respond, "Just let her keep trying."

Through the months of December and January, we incorporated classes back into Libby's schedule. She would take about two weeks to adjust to having this new class added to her routine. Once she'd settled in we'd add the next class with. Our goal was that she have all classes added back into her schedule by the beginning of the 3rd marking period. Biology and Lab were Libby's last classes for the day, so we all knew that our biggest leap into normalcy would be when Libby actually attended Mrs. Floorz class without Kelly or Mom helping out.

It was then that Kelly and I began to notice another problem with the school. Teachers forgot to turn in assignments to Guidance. Every day, before coming to the house, Kelly would go to the guidance office, turn in any assignments that Libby had finished and pick up new ones. We e-mailed all the teachers, reminding them that, even though Libby was now back in their class, Kelly was still willing to work on back or current assignments to help Libby get caught up with the rest of the class. Kelly's time at the house would be shortened each time we incorporated a class, but sometimes she would stay later in the day, willing to do whatever it took to see Libby succeed. Often for days on end there would be nothing waiting for Kelly at Guidance, so she'd come to the house, Libby would give her the assignments she'd remembered to write down and Kelly would help her with them, so tutoring wouldn't be a waste of time.

This became so frustrating because I'd then get five-week reports with teacher comments of *Work not done, incomplete or late* posted on most of her subjects. I would then e-mail each teacher asking them for the missing assignments and get sometimes two weeks worth of assignments in one e-mail. Both Kelly and I complained to Mr. King that teachers weren't handing in assignments, so how could they expect Libby to be on time or even catch up. Her report cards would carry two to three "**INC**" instead of grades because she was so far behind, yet, again and again, Kelly would come to the house empty handed.

After Christmas break, I e-mailed each teacher and said that within a few weeks Libby would be back in school full time and I would appreciate it if they each went through their assignment books to see what was missing. We wanted the transition of switching from having a tutor, to not having one, be a smooth one and we were trying hard at home to make sure Libby had all her assignments from each subject.

I thought Libby understood that by the beginning of February, Kelly would no longer be here to help her. We'd planned that Kelly would stay until after mid-term exams which were the end of January. So, on our visit to Dr. Rogers in January we discussed with him that Kelly would no longer be tutoring. I asked if he thought Libby was ready to take on a full day of school. I assured the doctor that I'd be there to help every evening with any homework or studying. I felt I was retaking freshman year along with my daughter and knew every assignment and test anyway.

I noticed that Libby seemed withdrawn during the doctor visit, even more than usual and once in the car, asked her if anything was wrong.

"None of you understand," she said, bursting into tears. "You're all turning your back on me and don't believe anything I say!"

I sat, not saying anything, listening to her sobs and realized that this was because she now understood that Kelly would be leaving. There was nothing I could do to help her. Somehow she'd have to figure out that she could do this. I'd still be there to help. It was another change in her routine and obviously she didn't feel ready for it.

We made it through mid-term exams. The day finally came when Libby started her first full day of school, Feb.1, 2007, over four months after her accident. While Kelly was still here, we hounded every teacher with e-mails insisting that they go through their records and make sure Libby was completely caught up in each of their classes. Again the majority was cooperative and the first week of school seemed to be going smoothly. I had just a couple calls from her and seemed to be able to reassure her that she could do it, because I didn't have to get her once from school.

Thursday, Libby came home from school, visibly upset. She'd received a detention in Biology. It was for not having her assignments completed on time or not done. Thinking this must be a mistake I got on the computer and e-mailed Mrs. Floorz, asking her for an explanation. No mistake about it. Libby hadn't turned in labs that had been due weeks before. I went back through all my e-mails and didn't find a single lab that Mrs. Floorz had not received except one that needed to be done under a microscope. Knowing Libby couldn't see through one, Mrs. Floorz had postponed this lab until she found projector slides that Libby could look at instead.

Sure enough, when I wrote back that we didn't have any labs on record as not being completed, that lab was included along with three others that had been due from four weeks before to two weeks before Libby was to start back to school full time. When I reminded Mrs. Floorz that I'd sent her repeated e-mails asking for any late work and she hadn't even given us the other labs yet, her response was, "Then she can make them up in detention. It's not really a punishment, but a way to insure that my students won't slack off and not get these labs done."

How insulting. I reminded her in my next e-mail that she could word it any way she wanted but "detention" was a punishment and Libby didn't deserve to be punished. This was Libby's first full week back to school in almost five months. The last thing she needed was to feel she'd done something wrong. On top of that, she'd have her day extended another hour. There was no changing Mrs. Floorz' mind. She insisted on Libby staying after school for detention. I then told her I'd be there too since I had been Libby's lab partner through all her other labs. I called Mr. King, which was a waste of time, since I got his all too familiar answer, "I'll look into it and get back to you."

Our "detention" was extremely quiet, considering Libby had to make up four labs. We worked on the labs while Mrs. Floorz sat at her desk and stayed out of the way. We passed a few looks, hers smug and mine cold, but managed to pass the hour without another argument.

I really tried to understand this teacher. I did understand that Regents courses in New York State have requirements that have to be met before the student can pass, but I've studied the regent's requirements online, (I never did get them from Mrs. Floorz). I found that Libby had actually met her hourly requirement in labs even before 3rd marking period began. This requirement was met just in Libby's make up labs after school, even before she started back to classes' full time. All the time I'd been asking for the exact hours needed, trying to make sure that Libby would complete them in time to take her final exam, what I really found was that most of the supposed requirements were minimal. I wouldn't have had to push Libby as hard by dragging her down to the school several times a week, for several hours at a time.

Everything this teacher did got under my skin and in all honesty probably everything I did got under hers. She was not the enemy. She didn't injure my daughter physically, but her uncaring attitude, and constant reminder that Libby wasn't going to pass her class, became the object of my anger. Several times, she lost Libby's work and rather than look harder for it, would suggest to us that Libby do it again. She even had the audacity to suggest that since Libby had memory issues it must be her fault. Thank God Kelly kept a log of every assignment and signed the log daily as she turned these assignments in to Guidance.

One afternoon after school, I had a rare moment of quiet. Libby was in her room sleeping and for the first time in a long time I turned on the television. My favorite talk show host/ comedian was on and she was announcing her guests for the show. She mentioned a husband and wife with names I wasn't familiar with, but her next words stopped me in my tracks. She began to explain that "Bob Woodruff", a popular news anchor, had sustained a severe traumatic brain injury while covering a story in Iraq. Bob and his wife Lee would be on the show to talk about their experience.

When they were finally on, I couldn't stop listening. Here was a man who had spent months in a coma, had a very visual injury to the side of his skull, had learned to walk and talk all over again, and was still obviously having some difficulties with his speech. When Lee Woodruff started explaining all they'd been through and some of the things that Bob was now doing, such as forgetting words, having trouble with his emotions, forgetting all sorts of things, I began to see Libby and as Lee ticked off the list of impairments, I mentally thought to myself. "She does that, and that, and that…" Bob didn't have a concussion; he had a full blown, devastating traumatic brain injury that had almost killed him.

If all of that was true, and Libby hadn't even been considered serious, with only Dr. Rogers calling her injury a TBI, then why was my daughter experiencing those same symptoms? I found it hard to believe that my daughter and this man could share so many of the same issues, but they did.

I watched Lee, a very animated speaker, as she listed all these impairments, keep a smile on her face, while optimism just oozed from her demeanor. Something she said confused or upset Bob. He leaned forward, scowling, as if he wanted to say something or ask his wife something. Without missing a beat, Lee reached out her hand in comfort and touched her husband. He leaned back, content that she was in control. Whatever issue he had or whatever he wanted to say, seemed to evaporate as his eyes connected with his wife.

That single touch, that hand on his thigh, that gesture of comfort, suddenly opened my eyes to the reality of what we were living at home. I don't know how many times I'd touched Libby in that very same way, whenever I'd see that troubled look come into her eyes. It is an unconscious thing that women do. To reach out in comfort, assuring that it's OK, we'll take care of it. Almost every time Libby and I exchanged that same gesture, she too, would lean back, knowing that Mom was in control, even when she wasn't.

For the first time since Libby's accident, I grieved. I cried for the child who for fourteen years had lived with us. Our lives had meshed and blended so smoothly. Now everything was chaos. I cried for the child who now lived with us, that girl I didn't really know or understand. I felt helpless. I sat watching this woman on the television as she smiled and, described the months in intensive care. I wondered if we'd ever smile again.

Finally, I began to understand just a little of what Dr. Rogers had been trying to tell us. Our daughter was now a different person.

I decided that, from this point on, I was done with the term "concussion". I now truly understood that my daughter had traumatic brain injury. Our lives were different because of it. It didn't matter how she got it or that she was never in a coma. Libby had a TBI and somehow we'd find the strength to heal. I now also understood that my daughter would make it too. If this family could smile, then someday, so would we.

CHAPTER 7

"Hey Look Llamas"

Just when we would think we'd understand TBI, something would happen to remind us how little we really knew. Every day, when Libby still had her tutor, I'd pick her up at school and drive her home. There's about a six mile stretch of country road before climbing our hill to home, and on that stretch of road is an Alpaca farm. The owners had recently bought these beautiful, gentle, wide eyed creatures and decided to try raising and breeding them. They'd started their farm just a couple of months before Libby's accident. We also had a neighbor on the other side of the hill that had raised Llamas for years.

One sunny day in December, the Alpaca's were out in their pastures and as we drove by, Libby smiled and pointed. "Hey, look, Llamas."

"They're Alpacas, Honey, aren't they adorable?"

"Oh Mom, they're so cute. How long have they been there?" We were now past the farm and I put my signal on to turn onto our road.

"I'm not sure. I think they've been there for a couple months," I said, concentrating on driving.

"Oh, I never noticed them before." Libby twisted in her seat so she could keep watching them.

We drove home in silence, but later that day, Libby asked me the difference between Llamas and Alpacas and we talked about our other neighbor who had Llamas named Pepsi and Coke and about some of the differences.

I didn't think any more about our conversation, until a couple days later, as we drove by the farm again Libby exclaimed excitedly, "Hey, look, Llamas!"

"Honey, they're Alpacas, remember?" I looked at her suspiciously.

"Oh," was all she said.

Another week went by and we drove by the farm again. "Hey, Mom, look Llamas!" Libby voice was filled with excitement.

"Are you joking?" I asked loosing my patience, remembering the past week and our conversations.

"No, look, really, they're back there," she pointed innocently as we drove past the farm. "How long have they been there?"

I took a deep breath, put what I thought was a smile on my face, and once again had the conversation about them being Alpacas and not Llamas. I explained that Bob had Llamas and Sam had the Alpacas. I went into a detailed description about the differences thinking that, just maybe, she'd absorb the fact that we drive by this Alpaca farm every day and she doesn't remember it being there. Apparently my voice carried the tension I was feeling.

"Are you mad at me?" Those wide, brown, innocent eyes watched me carefully.

Was I? I wasn't really sure, if I was honest with myself. Why was I having this same conversation over and over with her? Why couldn't she just remember?

So I lied. "No Honey, I'm not mad. I'm just tired."

"Oh," she said eying me suspiciously. She didn't believe me.

Was this conversation now over or was it going to turn into tears and a meltdown? Libby leaned back in her seat, closed her eyes and sighed. I didn't want to be angry. I felt guilty because I was. I tried to reason with myself and say that I wasn't really angry at her, but at what had happened to her, making her this way. It didn't work. She knew. I felt guilty, feeling the way I did. She was my daughter, that beautiful baby I gave birth to, not a stranger.

Another week went by before the Alpacas were out again. The weather had been nasty and it was the first sunny day. I noticed them frolicking around in their pastures. I looked at Libby to see if she would notice them. She looked right at them, but never said a word.

"Yeaaaaa, she must have finally remembered them," I thought to myself.

The next day, as we were driving past, I noticed that the Alpacas were still out, so I decided to tempt fate. I pointed them out to her. "Look, Libby, the Alpacas are out again today."

"What?" She looked at me blankly.

"The Alpacas, they were out playing today," I said again, watching her.

"What Alpacas?" She asked again.

My heart plummeted as I started the conversation that was now becoming all too familiar to me. She listened, while I chatted on the way home, and simply shrugged without comment.

A couple days later, on a nice sunny day we drove by again. "Hey look Llamas." I heard Libby's voice from the passenger side of the car.

I couldn't do this again. I couldn't explain one more time. "Yep," I said without saying another word. And so it went for weeks on end, as Libby would exclaim in excitement about the Llamas and I stayed silent, just nodding an affirmative, without having any more discussions.

On our next doctor visit, I explained the Llama situation to Dr. Perry telling her about the farm and how we drive by it and that Libby didn't remember it being there.

"Mom, I do too," Libby said angrily. "I know Bob has Llamas; he's had them for a long time."

We ended up having the same conversation about Alpacas and Llamas in front of Dr. Perry. I explained to Libby about the Alpaca farm and what she said when we drove by them. Libby's comment was, "Oh, how long have they been there?"

"I think, when you see Dr. Rogers next time, you should bring this up and see if he has any suggestions," our family physician said.

So I did. We had our monthly appointment the very next day. I began telling him about the Alpaca farm and that Libby would always start out by saying "Hey, look, Llamas." Libby immediately jumped in.

"Mom, Bob has Llamas not Alpacas." She was visibly angry at me. "I'm not stupid." Why do you treat me like I am?" She was nearing tears, but I had to have this conversation through to the end so Dr. Rogers could understand.

"Libby, I don't think you're stupid. It's just that there are two farms and you can only remember one of them. There's one farm on our way home from school that has Alpacas and every time we drive by, you don't remember that you've seen them before or that they're Alpacas."

Immediately, Libby pulled into her defensive shell and stopped talking. She'd been cuddling with me on the couch, but pulled away scooting to the other side, shooting looks of betrayal my way. I looked at Dr. Rogers for help. He shrugged saying the brain was tricky. He suggested possibly stopping at the farm to get a more concrete memory for Libby, such as a hands on experience.

The next morning, I called the family and asked if it would be possible to stop by some day so Libby could see the Alpacas. Terri was very understanding when I told her what had been happening. She said "Stop by anytime."

For the next week the Alpacas weren't out. Finally we started our January thaw and the weather warmed. As we drove by, I could see that the Alpacas were out, so I pointed them out to Libby.

She seemed excited. Instantly she talked about them being Llamas. As we got a little closer, I could see people walking around in the pasture and decided that this was the day, so I pulled into their driveway.

"What are you doing? Do you know these people?"

"Yes, Libby, we know them. You go to school with Sam and I know his mom. She said we could stop and see them any time, so let's get out and see if we can pet one."

"Oh, wow, really? What about Kelly? We'll be late. What if she gets there before we do?" This was again out of our routine and I could see the panic building in her face.

"Well, we'll only stay a minute." I promised.

Terri saw us and met us at the gate. Smiling, she let us in, all the while talking about how much she loved these animals, and how much fun they were and how shy they were. Libby looked around at all the Alpacas and naturally, picked out the one that had a baby. Terri went over, cradled her arms around the little, one and guided him to Libby so she could pet it. Shyly, Libby pets the pretty cocoa brown baby, not saying a word.

I explained that we couldn't stay long. After a few minutes of letting Libby love on the baby, I thanked Terri for her hospitality and we left. Libby didn't say much on the way home, but finally made the connection between Sam at school and that this was his farm.

It worked. Never again did we drive by the farm and hear Libby say "Hey, look, Llamas". For weeks, I held my breath waiting, and one time just to test her I said "Hey, look, Llamas" as we drove by only to get a scowl from Libby.

"Mom they're not Llamas, Bob has Llamas, they're Alpacas."

So OK, the memory of the farm was now in her brain to stay, but Libby never remembered the daily conversations that we used to have about Llamas. That's OK; she doesn't need to remember that.

CHAPTER 8

The new normal

It's such a weird feeling waking up every morning and instead of thinking about what to do on the farm today, to think about Libby. I hope that this day will be better for her than the day before. I pray that something else will come back to her to make her life just a little easier. I sit down and read through the agenda I've started keeping or sit and write in my journal. I have had to learn how to organize. No, not just organize, but micro manage every detail. My agenda and journal keep me together, trudging along with all the changes and things I now have to help Libby remember.

Our farm almost ceased to exist. Dave and I decided it was just too much to try to keep up with horses and what Libby was going through at the same time. Gradually one by one, we sold off every horse except my stallion, Aaran, Libby's mare, Mable, and her foal, Mozart. We kept Aaran and Mable for sentimental reasons, still clinging to the past, hoping there still might be something we could salvage, once this nightmare was over. Mozart was Libby's. We had no plans on selling him in the hopes that some day, she'd recover enough to go to the barn and start working with him again. They reminded us of better times. We weren't quite ready to let go.

Mozart was now a yearling. He had just the basic halter breaking when he was a new foal. Since then, he had barely been touched. Libby hardly went to the barn anymore. She used to go to Mable and cry out her troubles, burying her head in her mares' neck. Now, instead, she went to bed. She used to be interested in the kittens that were born occasionally in the barn, but two litters had come and gone, without Libby paying any attention to them.

By February, Libby was back in school full time; Kelly no longer came every afternoon. I helped with homework now. I was still getting calls from school when her days got too bad and I'd have to go get her. Those days, once she was home Libby slept. No homework got done. That meant e-mailing each teacher and explaining that homework would again be late.

We were starting to get Phase I letters because Libby was missing so much school. Our school policy was if a student misses so many days of school, the parents are sent Phase I letters as a warning. If they miss five more days the parents get a Phase II letter explaining that regardless of the grade the student is in jeopardy of not getting credit for that class. I was assured by Mrs. Crabner that as long as Libby made up those days by completing the work, she would make sure Libby got credit for the class, but the Phase I, and even a couple Phase II, letters continued to come as the school year came to a close.

We'd made it through our first depositions with our lawsuit. The school's attorney deposed Libby, Dave and I. Frank questioned the two bus drivers. I now realized that the lawsuit really wasn't accomplishing what I'd hoped at school. I was still trying to reason with the school, begging them for some type of accommodations that would still allow Libby to work at a slower pace, without being penalized. I had formed good relationships with Libby's English, Global and Spanish teachers. We maintained our weekly e-mail and they worked around Libby's impairments. Biology continued to be a thorn in our side and Math now was taking over as our leading problem. Libby still struggled with Algebra, some days understanding it and others not. Her grades were borderline failing. I couldn't help because I'd never taken algebra, but had concentrated on business courses when I was in high school.

Libby asked her Math teacher, several times, if she could stay after school for extra help with no results. Once she'd actually been told by the teacher. "Pffft, it's a Friday are you kidding?"

Libby was now having another problem. In the past Kelly turned in Libby's assignments. Now she had to try to remember to do it herself. Many times Libby and I worked on an assignment together, only to have her put it in her book bag and completely forget about it. So even though she did the work, she didn't remember to turn it in. Her focus was so poor that, if she was occupied by getting out her text book, she wouldn't even hear the teacher ask for the assignments or notice tomorrow's assignment written on the board.

Other times, she would forget that she had an assignment at all. So even though her amnesia was diminishing, we were now finding that her short term memory was taking over as the leading culprit in impairments.

In Global, one morning, Libby noticed that the other students were handing work forward. She asked what it was, only to find out it was an assignment sheet she'd been given the day before. The teacher wasn't in the room yet, so Libby quickly tried to fill in answers. Two well meaning friends started helping and gave her some of their answers, just so she wouldn't be behind again for the umpteenth time. When Mr. Matthews walked in and caught them, they all received zeros for that day.

That evening, Libby and I were doing homework on the PC and she started telling me about what had happened that morning. All of a sudden she clutched the arms of the loveseat she was sitting in and got a funny look on her face.

"What's the matter?" Thinking that it was something about getting in trouble, I waited. She didn't move, but continued to look off into space, with a look of pure panic in her eyes. "Libby what's wrong? Are you having a panic attack?" She didn't move or acknowledge I was there. She was still for several minutes, while I grew more and more afraid. Then a little glimmer came into her eyes and she began blinking and looking around. I watched as she slowly picked up the pen she'd dropped and stared at it. She moved it to her other hand, still staring at it like it was a totally foreign object.

"This is weird," she whispered. "What hand to I write with?"

"Your right," I said, studying her, waiting to see where this was going.

For a couple of seconds, she switched the pen from hand to hand then picked up a slip of paper and wrote,

"My name Is Li
   Bby my moms name
    is Na
     Omi".

I looked at the writing. It reminded me of the first day she tried to write and couldn't.

What just happened, Libby?" I watched her closely.

"I don't know." Her speech was slow and a little slurred. "I could hear you talking and then this buzzing started in my head. I could still hear you but it was way off, like you were far away." She was looking at the paper she'd written on and shook her head. "This happened to me before." Her voice was quiet and emotionless.

"When," I asked? Great, we were just getting used to long term and short term memory problems and now we have this, what ever this is.

"I don't remember," Libby began, still speaking slowly, but a little clearer. "At school," she said, brightening, because she remembered where. "Yep, at school. I remember sitting at my desk in Bio and feeling this, but afterward I couldn't read my Biology book."

Then she burst into tears. "What's wrong with me Mom?" She reached out for me and I grabbed her hand.

"I don't know, honey, but we'll find out." I assured her, all the while feeling just as afraid as she was.

"Am I dying?" she asked.

"Oh, no, Baby," I said and gathered her in my arms. I could feel her trembling as she clung to me tightly. "You are not dying! In fact, you're getting better every day." I stroked her hair and thought about how much easier this used to be when I could gather her on to my lap. It was so simple back then. Libby sobbed for a while, and I let her cry until her sobs quieted to hic-ups.

"I don't feel like I'm getting better," she said, no longer sobbing, but still sniffling. "I try to pretend I am, but inside I still feel like nothing's getting better."

"Libby, do you know how proud I am of you?" I said, stroking her hair.

"Every morning I watch you go to school and know that you don't know where you're going, who your friends are, or even if you can read that day, but you still get up and you still walk out that door." She looked up at me not understanding, with those ever expressive eyes. "You are the bravest person I know." I said, looking directly into her eyes. "Honestly, I don't know if I could get up like you do and go to school every day, not knowing if you'll remember what you need to."

A little glimmer of understanding registered in her deep brown eyes and she smiled just a little. "So I'm not going to die?"

I sighed deeply and gathered her back into my arms. "No, honey, you aren't going to die." I kissed the top of her head as tears welled up in my own eyes. "You're going to live to be a very old lady with a hundred cats running around her house." I could feel her smiling against my chest.

"Can I tell you something?" Her voice was muffled against my chest and she squeezed me tightly.

"You can tell me anything!" I assured her.

"Well, you know how I keep asking you to sleep with me?" She looked up at me, no longer smiling.

"Yea, I know," I said squeezing her a little. "Daddy keeps asking me when I'm going to sleep in my own bed again."

She shrugged a little, not really concerned about Dad's feelings at that moment.

"Yea, well, the reason I want you to sleep with me is because I don't want to die alone."

I gasped. "Oh, honey, I promise you aren't going to die!"

"But all those tests I've had and all the doctors, and I know I'm not acting right, but I can't help it, and now this buzzing thing."

I couldn't hold back the tears, my baby, my little girl had no idea whether she was going to live or die. She was going to bed silently, every night, wondering if this was going to be her last. She didn't have enough of a clear thought process yet to know that she was slowly getting better. She could only see the negative.

The next morning I contacted Libby's neurologist and she ordered an EEG thinking possibly that she could be experiencing mini mall seizures. Apparently, once the swelling in the brain goes down, occasionally it leaves scar tissue that can cause seizures. This usually occurs four to six months post injury. The EEG came back normal, so once again we were left with no answers. The spells, as we began to call them, continued on, sporadically, adding just one more thing for all of us to worry.

Two years after Libby experienced her spells; we had an explanation why nothing showed up on her testing. The doctors have now found that damage can happen in the white matter surrounding the brain. White matter damage doesn't show up on conventional scans or MRI's. They now had new technology available that might actually show the damage to the white matter, but only a few hospitals in the Nation had this technology at their disposal.

During all this, my son, Tony, was getting married the first week of March. It was going to be a simple ceremony because it was both Tony and his fiancé's second marriage. When Libby was seven, Tony had married a young woman, who was fresh out of high school, and already had a son. They were both young, didn't know what they wanted out of life yet and moved to Florida for a few years. They had two daughters together, then moved back to New York, when their marriage began failing. When the marriage ended, Tony moved in with us for a while. He got custody of all three kids. Eventually a permanent custody agreement was arranged where they shared custody and finalized their divorce. Jackie came into the family quietly and happily, willing to take on the mother role and after dating for over a year they set their wedding date for March 3rd.

Jackie was a welcome addition to our family. In all honesty, most of what was going on in Tony and Peyton's' lives became secondary, until we could get control of our new way of life with Libby. We still attended birthday parties and all the important functions, but those little every day things, like first home runs, and A+'s on report cards, slipped by Dave and me.

Both boys quietly watched what we went through, with little comment, each handling it his own way. Peyton was married with two daughters and a new baby son that was just learning how to walk. They were supportive but distant. They came occasionally to see us, but they were on the outside of what was happening in our home now. They too struggled with the changes they saw in their sister.

The first time Libby went to Peyton and Camille's home after her accident, she remembered them and their children, but didn't remember they had a huge yellow lab named Rueben. Libby and Rueben had been best buddies, so naturally when Libby sat on the sofa, Rueben came over and put his face in Libby's, almost touching noses with her. She cringed away from him and cried out in fear, as Peyton grabbed Rueben and pulled him away. Peyton looked physically ill; as the realization came to him that his baby sister didn't know his dog. It was a real eye opener to her oldest brother.

At first, Peyton joked with Libby, naturally thinking she'd recover like he did. Once she didn't, he didn't want to face that his sister may now have a permanent disability. He'd get harsh sometimes and accuse her of faking it just to get our attention, which would break Libby's heart. In time, Peyton came to realize that some of the old Libby was still there. As she improved and regained some of her sense of humor, Peyton was once again the one to joke with her, coming up to her and shaking her hand saying "Hi, I'm your big brother. Remember me?" He'd usually get an "Oh, ha-ha very funny," from Libby and a smile.

The boys were the first ones to actually begin treating Libby normally again. Peyton, by joking and calling it the way he saw it, and Tony, with his actions. Peyton was always the talker and Tony was our quiet, but busy son.

One sunny day in late February, Tony pulled in with his truck, hauling a trailer with a snowmobile. He proceeded to unload the snowmobile, while my grandson ran to the house, all grins, telling how his Dad just bought a new sled and he was going to get to ride on it. Off they went as soon as the sled was unloaded. They came back about an hour later. When they came in, I gave them each a hot cocoa and listened to Tony tell about his new toy.

Libby looked out the door and asked "Can you give me a ride?" Before I had a chance to say a big NO, he said, "Sure, get your coat." She ran for her room. It was the fastest I'd seen her move in a long time.

"Tony, be very careful, her neck and back are still bad…"

"Chill, Mom, I'm just going to take her in the field and I'll be careful," he said, grinning at me as he handed Libby the extra helmet. I got that crooked grin of his and with a twinkle in his eyes he said, "*I PROMISE!*" Before I could say any more, they were out the door. He was there for her, later that year, when she decided to try to get back on Mable for the first time, encouraging her and picking on her in that big brother way. He saw his sister who used to be fearless on a horses back, now clinging to Mable's mane and not remembering anything about how to ride a horse.

While we were starting to get used to our new way of life, life just kept happening around us. We were slowly learning that we only had ourselves to depend on, while the immediate and extended family had to learn that Libby may not get back to their idea of "normal". It was hard watching what I thought was a close knit family struggle with getting to know Libby as the new Libby and trying to be cheerful with Dave and me. In all honesty, cheerfulness wasn't always what we needed. Sometimes we just needed our parents and sisters and brothers to say "Wow, this is awful, what can we do to help?"

I have a loving caring mother who raised four daughters, practically on her own. Though she would listen to me some days, as I cried my heart out about what was happening to my baby, she would then say something about Libby and "when she gets back to normal" or "when she gets all better." Finally, one day, when we were over at Grandma's house, Libby was playing a board game with Mom. Libby had the score pad and was trying to add up their score, when she wrote the numbers backwards and couldn't add.

Mom never said a word, but later that day, she called me in tears saying "I didn't understand, Naomi; I never understood really when you were talking to me."

I listened quietly, while my mother cried, as she came to the realization that she'd have to learn to love our new Libby, just as she was. If she got better wonderful, and if she didn't, that had to be OK too. I had now moved to the phase that you hope and pray for a full recovery, but plan for what was happening today, because we just didn't know what tomorrow would be.

My father, though I loved him dearly, wasn't in our immediate lives. He and my mother had divorced when I was in my early twenties and he'd moved to Florida with his second wife. The year before Libby's accident, they, too, separated and Dad had started calling his daughters again. He'd been diagnosed with Bi-polar Disorder when he was in his forties. He was an alcoholic for as long as I could remember. Dad had a tendency to call, when he was manic, and demand the attention of whichever daughter he thought might cooperate with his schemes. He was wrapped up in finalizing his divorce. I honestly don't think he comprehended the seriousness of Libby's condition.

In February of 2007, Dad began calling me in the morning, demanding I go and look for papers he thought pertinent to his divorce. At the same time I was getting calls from the school because Libby has having a meltdown. I tried explaining to my Dad that today wasn't a good day and that I might need to go to school to get Libby. Apparently, the school lost her and had put on a search, calling me to come and help. When I explained to Dad that I couldn't talk, he became furious and hung up.

After finding Libby in one of the practice rooms in orchestra, I gathered her up and took her home, only to find that Dad had called seventeen times. Our last conversation we ever had was in anger. He never called me again. I told myself that I would give Dad a call when Libby didn't need so much of my attention. My dad passed away before we resolved our differences.

Libby's friends had slowly stopped calling except for one friend from school and her cousin Kiara. To Kiara, it never seemed to matter and she accepted Libby just as she was today, and whatever tomorrow brought, that would be OK too. She was Libby's support line at school, her confidant and sometimes it seemed, her only real friend. The other girls sometimes didn't understand that "girl chat" meant nothing to Libby right now. Boyfriends were beyond her comprehension too. When the girls would start to chatter about this or that, often Libby would just stop them with a (not so polite) "Quiet! You're making my head hurt!"

Gradually, as they matured and Libby didn't, they moved on, continuing doing what teenagers do. Libby's best friend Claire would come to the house sometimes, but she'd started dating. Libby just didn't seem interested in boys or what Claire was doing, so gradually, for a while even she too stopped calling.

But Kiara stuck it out and took the bad with the good. The two girls had grown up together. My sister had Kiara six months before Libby was born. It was inevitable that they were going to be best friends. They shared the same crib, blankets on the floor and childhood family memories. So, when those memories were sketchy for Libby, Kiara would help fill in the blanks.

She was the first one Libby giggled with, once her memories started coming back, and the first one to spend the night after the accident. She was Libby's anchor in her world, outside of Mom and Dad and home. Kiara encouraged her to get out there and do things again, once Libby started to regain some of her strength.

Dave and I too found that our circle of friends had changed. Our old friends who'd kept inviting us out to dinner, finally stopped after the twentieth time of explaining how we just couldn't leave Libby alone yet. We'd tried a couple of times, only to find she'd left the stove on while we were gone, or sometimes we'd only be gone a half an hour when Libby would call, in a panic, because she couldn't remember where we said we were going. Eventually, most of the people, except our families, just stopped calling and asking. That hurt, but we tried to understand. We could no longer keep up with their world, so they moved on.

Within a short time, we found others, good hearted people who were just willing to come to the house instead of going out. Those same people included Libby in an invitation to come to their home. If we had to stop and deal with a meltdown, they were patient and understood. Dave and I began to have Friday night card night at the house and our group of eight to ten people gathered for a hearty game of Texas hold-em, Euchre, or whatever we felt like. Willy and Rebecca, Collin and Christine, and occasionally their teenage daughter Pam, along with Matt, Alex and Jessica showed us that life goes on.

Rebecca was a mother hen around Libby, always making sure she was included. She would sit with Libby and show her how to make quilted scrapbook covers, while we played cards at the other table.

"Shooo, she'd say to me smiling." Go on, Libby and I have everything under control, you go play cards."

I found I could relax again and laugh at Collins antics, as he picked on his wife Christine. Willy was always keeping Dave and me laughing and I could see, that as much as Rebecca gave me that break from mothering, Willy gave Dave back some semblance of normalcy, too, as he picked on Dave's card playing abilities. Matt, though a little younger, came and joked with Libby, picking on her like a brother. Alex and Jessie came when they could because Jessie was a traveling nurse and Alex sometimes had guard duty at the prison he worked at. They all became a part of our new normal.

Once in a while, Christine's daughter, Pam, would come to the house when she was visiting for the weekend. Pam lived with Christine's ex-husband during school and would visit Collin and Chris every chance she could get. She was a couple of years younger than Libby, but they seemed to hit if off right away. Pam would encourage Libby to be silly and it didn't matter if Libby didn't feel well, Pam would just read a book and be quiet with Libby, when that was what she needed.

As others joined our Friday night group, gradually we'd find them either becoming a part of our new family, or after a couple nights, they'd just stop coming. It was OK with us. Dave and I needed to surround ourselves with people who accepted us just the way we were. If someone new came for the evening, I'd give a brief explanation that sometimes we had to take Libby breaks, and if they were uncomfortable with it, they just stopped coming. Very slowly our lives were coming back to a semblance of normal. We were learning to adjust. Libby was starting to find herself again and little by little we began to see signs of recovery.

When Pam was around, we began to see a little of the old Libby. She would rush into the dining room, where we played cards, teasing for Pam to spend the night. Christine was great and would let Pam stay almost every time. Pam made Libby feel that life was returning again. Libby didn't always just have to work on remembering. She could laugh and be silly, or watch a movie. If she didn't understand something, Pam took on the big sister role and would calmly explain, as if it was the most natural thing in the world.

There were a few times, though, when Pam stayed, that Libby continued to sleep while Pam wandered around the living room, waiting for her to wake up. I explained to her that sometimes Libby just needed to sleep. From then on, if Pam stayed, she brought a book to read or found something else to do. It never seemed to bother Pam that Libby wasn't always attentive to her.

It seemed without question, our new friends just accepted what was, for the day, and since that was the only way Dave and I knew how to live anymore, it worked out perfectly for us. Sometimes I have to stop and think about something and realize that some things about Libby's accident had become blessings in disguise. If Libby had never been hurt, we'd probably never have become friends with some of the most interesting, fun, crazy, characters we've come across in our thirty years of marriage.

It became just a little easier to be in our own skins again and accept what life had thrown at our family. Those few hours, we didn't have to think about what problems were at school, or if Libby had a good or bad week, we could just relax. It's so important to find that something that keeps you going, when life gets you down. It's so easy to get caught up in all the problems, doctor appointments, expectations of others that you can no longer fulfill. Take just a few hours, no matter what it takes, to do that for yourself, to just be human again and surround yourself with people who don't expect perfection from you, but are just willing to take you and your life as it is. It's so easy to burn out emotionally, when for twenty four hours a day, every day, you have to be on your toes, expecting the unexpected, foreseeing the unforeseen, heading off emotional storms, keeping track of what's going on at school, at the lawyers, at the doctors and at home. Good friends are so important. At a time in our life when we couldn't reciprocate, they were just friends to us.

Watching Libby lose most of her friends at school was so hard to watch. It was so rewarding when she began making new friends. These friends didn't know the old Libby, only who she was now, so it didn't matter and she didn't have to try to be somebody she no longer was.

For a time, Dave and I went through a period where we just had to say "The Hell with the rest of the world." It included anyone who just didn't fit into our new way of life. We were forced to accept what had happened in our family. If the outside world couldn't accept that, then "move on". We just didn't have the energy to deal with any one else's problems. I know that sounds extremely selfish and maybe it was, but it was necessary. It was the only way we knew how to survive and keep our immediate family intact.

CHAPTER 9

Hope

Glimmers of hope come in all shapes and sizes. Our first real evidence that we could cling to was when final exams came. I'd been dreading them because Libby struggled so all year long. This would show that either we were right in pushing her so hard, after they'd suggesting pulling classes, or the school was. I know, maybe not the healthiest way to look at things, but by the end of the year, I felt that battle lines had been drawn between school administration and our family. If Libby could just pass her finals, everything she worked so hard for would have been worthwhile. Even if she had to retake her Biology Regents' exam later, I was fine with that, because I knew Libby had done her best. The last two marking periods, she'd received failing grades in Biology. I no longer held out much hope of her passing the course.

In Spanish, Mr. Martinez let her come in after class. He broke down all the conversations she would have to memorize for his final. He let her practice one line, repeat it from memory, and then practice the next and repeat that until she had fulfilled all his requirements to pass his course. He let her do some collage boards for extra credit and seemed fine with her passing, but did suggest to us that, possibly, she might want to skip Spanish next year. For not remembering a word of Spanish, Libby's final average was an 85.

She received some failing grades in Math, but got an 80 on the final, which brought her grade up to passing. In early spring, we found a wonderful man who tutored Libby once a week in Algebra. After Gerry began helping Libby, her Math grade average improved by ten points. In Global, she stayed steady in the low 70's all through school, mainly because this was one of her early classes and Libby had been able to be in Mr. Matthew's class throughout most of the year. For English, it was the same. Low grades, but passing. Orchestra and Choir never got below a 96, even through the hardest part of her recovery. During Phys-Ed, I'd helped Libby with essays on each sport they covered, while she was being tutored and had limited Phys-Ed once she returned. Once again, Libby received all passing grades.

For Biology, I cried for joy. Libby got an 80 on her Biology regents, but a 62 for her last marking period. Her final exam pulled her grade average up to a 72 and she passed! With everything that happened throughout the school year, my daughter had passed every course. She was moving on to 10th grade still in mainstream education, with the possibility of a Regent's diploma.

It no longer mattered that I'd sat with her every evening, helping her with her homework, sometimes typing out her essays from her rough draft for her because it took her so long to type. All the fights with teachers, the begging and pleading and smiling when I wanted to cry, paid off. I have to stop and give Libby so much credit. She didn't give up. She kept trudging away and she did it!

Another ray of hope came when Libby had her neuropsych testing done. It was a full day of one test after another. She came out of the testing exhausted and with a huge migraine, but she completed all the tests. The results weren't great, but not horrible, either. Each test pointed to several impairments that directly related to her TBI. Libby took these tests eight months after her accident. Finally we had something concrete that we could take to the school and say, "See, this is where she needs assistance." I'd requested that Libby be reviewed for accommodations in her school, even going so far as writing a letter asking the school to test her if it meant helping her. Even after completing her entire freshman year, no accommodations had been put into place. We discussed this with Dr. Rogers, and decided not to push the school into any accommodations until after the results came back on her neuropsych testing. I got those results two weeks after school was over for the summer.

In April, I'd been searching the internet for information on TBI and came across a web page for the BIAA (Brain Injury Association of America). I saw that New York State had a chapter, BIANYS (Brain Injury Association of New York State). I contacted them, hoping that they could give me information on how to help Libby in school. Within twenty four hours, I'd been contacted by out next angel Sharon Johnson. Sharon was the FACTS (Family, Advocacy, Counseling, and Training Services) coordinator with BIANYS. Her job was to assist families of children with TBI's, through the school process and beyond school. She knew what programs were available for Libby, that might help her, and what she would and would not qualify for. I learned that hospitals or rehabilitation centers call on the BIAA when they receive a patient with head trauma. If the patient is twenty one or younger the FACTS Program is contacted. Because Libby hadn't been hospitalized, her name hadn't been give to BIANYS, but luckily I'd stumbled across their web site.

Immediately Sharon sent me information about the school process. I learned for the first time another important acronym, CSE (Committee for Special Education). The CSE is in every public school in America, there for parents of students with disabilities, yet not one single person in employment at our school district ever told me this department even existed. They determine if your child needs accommodations to their regular schooling. Things like longer times available for test taking, or special instructions that each teacher is supposed to follow that may help students. Libby certainly could use that. If the school had devised a system to remind her to turn in her homework, or write her assignments down, her grades would have been drastically different. Sharon sent several helpful booklets that walked us through the process. Within a week, she came to the house to meet us.

For the first time, I truly felt we weren't alone. A petite woman full of energy, personality and the nicest smile walked into our home and gave us hope. We could get through this. Sharon offered to come to any CSE meetings and felt sure that Libby would qualify for if not an IEP (Individualized Education Plan) at least a 504 Plan, which is a less rigid form of an IEP. Sharon also suggested a group called Parent to Parent, which is funded by New York. Parent to Parent helps put parents of children with disabilities in touch with other parents with similar circumstances. They also offered training seminars and workshops to those parents.

Through Parent to Parent, I attended a workshop that helps parents get ready for the CSE process, and it is a process. It's not easy; it's not simply telling your principal that you think your child needs help. Experts have written books for parents, just to help them understand the process and get through it successfully. At the workshop I met Sharon Marrella, Regional Director of Parent to Parent and Jean Tydings, Parent Coordinator and Advocate for The Advocacy Center. Both women put on the workshop, handed out several binders, one on the CSE process and one (Healthcare Notebook) that can help with keeping track of all the medical issues a child may have. I had no idea how important that binder would become to me, until I later began to use it and tailored it to our needs. This workshop was free of charge and was so helpful to me. I had never had to go through Special Education for anything at school before and obviously hadn't been very successful when it came to getting what Libby needed in the way of accommodations, in her freshman year. Our school never once said to me, "Mrs. Parker, to start the ball rolling you will need to write a letter to our Special Education Department. They will take care of everything."

Sharon and Jean showed our group how to come up with a Vision Plan for our children and how to be able to express it clearly. It didn't just say what the parent felt her child needed to be successful, but involved the child in the decision making process. A Vision Plan was something I'd sort of thought about in a non-committal way, but now it was concrete, in writing for me to look at. It actually made me feel that putting Libby's dreams down on paper made them more attainable, instead of impossible. Information in the binder involved our children and put them first. What do they need? What do they want? What don't they want? How we can make them more than a statistic. They suggested personalizing our binders with pictures of our children, so when we go into the CSE office, they aren't just a student, or a statistic of a certain illness or injury, but a real person, who has a personality of their own and needs all their own, too.

The evening of that workshop, I learned that The Advocacy Center would be there if we needed them, every step of the way. That was their job. They advocated for families, who were not having success on their own, in getting what their children needed. That night, I learned there was a class that The Advocacy Center offered, less than a half hour from my house. It would teach any parent who wanted to learn how to go through the CSE process successfully. The class would run from August through November.

I learned that, even though I'd written our principal and requested that Libby be tested and classified clear back in April, and had gotten no response from our district, that their lack of response was against regulations. Jean sat with me that evening and helped me write my first CSE letter. She suggested that I send it "Certified, Return Receipt Requested," and that I put "cc: Jean Tydings, The Advocacy Center" at the bottom. She smiled knowingly and just said, "Let's see how long it takes them to respond now."

I mailed my letter the first of August. I received not only a written response, but a phone call within forty eight hours, setting up our first CSE meeting.

When I spoke with the CSE chairperson, she let me know immediately that she had absolutely no knowledge of Libby, or that she'd been in an accident and that they didn't even have a file on her. She promised she'd contact the high school immediately and get what information she needed. I offered Libby's written diagnosis from Dr. Rogers and her neuropsych test as proof of disability and explained to the chairperson about all the e-mails and struggles we had gone through the past year. She assured me that this coming year would be different. That afternoon, I took a folder full of information down to the CSE office and handed it over personally. It contained copies of e-mails I'd kept from Biology and Math.

In mid August, I began my Advocacy classes. I can't begin to express how helpful they were. Classes were held every Thursday, for two months. It was a double edged sword, because the more I learned, the more I began to understand that what happened last year, in school, just never should have happened.

I learned by studying the part 200 Regulations from the Dept. of Education, that any school employee in their district has the ability, at any time, to refer a student to the CSE office for evaluation. In such cases as Libby's, when a student acquires a disability such as from an accident, the school district has the ability (but is not obligated) to put into place an emergency amendment, while that student recovers, allowing them do whatever is necessary to assure that the student doesn't fall behind. Our school could have allowed open book reading, testing and everything Dr. Rogers asked for in his letters. Instead we were ignored.

In Libby's case, they could have put a temporary amendment to her education that allowed for someone to read out loud to her, write for her, have open book testing, extended homework and test times while she recovered. I have to admit, some teachers did all that on their own, without school approval, and to them I will be eternally grateful.

Every state has its own set of regulations, but they are there. They are there for parents to look up and learn what their rights are and what their children's rights are. Most states have something like The Advocacy Center, too, though it may have a different name. The problem is that, unless someone tells us that this information is out there for us, we just don't know. The school certainly didn't offer any of this information to me, nor did they ever offer to walk me through the process.

While the school continued to tell me they could do nothing until she was classified, either they didn't know the regulations very well, or they outright lied to me. They could have had her evaluated at any time through their own psychologist, I'd given permission several times for them to do just that, and implement anything that Libby needed to succeed in 9th grade. Instead, they told me their hands were tied and they could do nothing. I'm sure this was in part due to the fact that we were suing the school district and any admission of injury would hurt their case.

When I started my advocacy training classes, there were seventeen other parents in various school districts throughout our county, all with their own set of issues and disabilities, but all with the same complaint. Why do their schools do nothing? Why is the fight so hard? Some parents already had a diagnosis, but were struggling with red tape. Some didn't have a diagnosis yet and were where I was with Libby in 9th grade. Some had been fighting for years and had finally pulled their child out of school and were now home schooling, because they felt they'd run out of options. Some were bitter and didn't hold out much hope that these classes could help, but were there anyway, just in case.

Each parent took turns telling her child's story. At first I felt guilty because I didn't think Libby's impairments were as severe as everyone else's child. She still played violin, was still in mainstream education. She might need a little assistance with her education, but nothing major. She wasn't considered severely handicapped. She wasn't in a wheelchair. She could speak, read and write again. With MTBI (Mild Traumatic Brain Injury) especially, the injury is so often cast aside as unimportant by people who don't understand and even by professionals who do. Most don't understand how devastating even a mild TBI can be and how much it can change a family's dynamics and especially how long it can take for recovery. When it was my turn to tell our story, and I began describing what we'd gone through for over a year, my feelings changed. I felt compassion and understanding from each parent. I even had several come up to me, after class, with encouraging words. I belonged here. Nobody else thought what we'd gone through was trivial or minor. Finally, here were people that understood.

For any parent who reads this, my advice to you is, grieve for your loss, don't try to diminish it by comparing it to anyone else's life. It's your life and your battle and your own unique set of circumstances. It's OK to be angry, it's OK to be sad, just don't give up.

I think there comes a time in each of our lives, when we have to face what has happened to our child and make a choice. Do we learn to fight constructively or give up and let the system bury our child in mounds of paper work and red tape?

I chose to fight. I just had to learn how to fight right. Instead of spewing anger and frustration for no reason at all, I had to learn to take my anger and make it become something positive. It was how I personally dealt with the now possibly permanent changes in my daughter. I heard Lee Woodruff on another talk show say this and it really struck home. "You can either get better or get bitter."

Sharon Johnson, Dave, Libby and I attended our first CSE meeting August 27, a week before Libby started her sophomore year. It was a whirlwind of information. The meeting included a teacher from last year, her coming year, our principal, the CSE chair, a secretary, the special education teacher for the high school, the school psychiatrist and a counselor named Jacob Myers.

We were told that, instead of e-mailing and dealing directly with each teacher, we could now go through Jacob and he'd make sure things got done. They promised this year would not be a repeat of last year and already had a tentative 504 Plan drawn up that included most of the accommodations I had requested, when I had turned in all the information, to CSE earlier that month. They took Dr. Rogers advice and implemented almost everything he suggested. There were almost no negative comments to anything I'd presented them in the folder. The committee also stated they were willing to accept Dr. Rogers testing, without testing Libby with their own psychologist, because the test I presented them was much more thorough than what they could do at the school.

Sandy Reynolds, the chairperson, started the meeting but quickly turned it over to Jacob. He apparently had Libby's "case file" and had done all the investigating as to why nothing had been put in place the previous year. We were never given a reason. As a matter of fact, that subject was avoided completely, but Jacob assured us that he would quickly handle anything that came along this year.

He began his speech with, "As you are all aware, Mr. & Mrs. Parker have a lawsuit pending with the school district, but I want to be open and up front about this and say that this shouldn't interfere with Elizabeth's education in any way."

He asked to counsel Libby and I was surprised, when she immediately spoke up and said, "NO WAY!"

Jacob assured us that he was very understanding about TBI's and could help her possibly with some strategies that she could use to make this year easier. So it was agreed that she would give him a chance. Two sessions were all Libby would concede to. She left the meeting saying she felt like they'd treated her like she didn't know anything. I was amazed at how fast and thorough the meeting was and Sharon commented that she'd never had one go so smoothly. We both smiled and agreed that advocacy classes were almost a necessity when going through the CSE process. It felt great to have some control once again.

When we got in the car, Libby mumbled, "I don't trust him."
"Who?"
"That Jacob guy, I don't trust him." She folded her arms across her chest and slumped down in the seat.

"C'mon, Libby, give him a chance. If he can keep the peace between us and the teachers, I don't want to do anything that will mess that up. Just try and give him a chance, OK?"

I'd had an uncomfortable moment when Jacob had talked about our lawsuit and wondered if it had been really necessary to bring it out into the open, but I wanted an advocate in the school, someone to finally fight for us and not against us so badly, I pushed that moment aside.

"I don't like him," she mumbled.

The following day I received my first e-mail from Jacob, assuring me that things would go much smoother and if I had any questions at all, to feel free to call or e-mail him. I returned an e-mail and let him know that he had a job ahead of him, gaining Libby's trust. I reminded him that he had just two chances to put her at ease. I didn't want to sugar coat it. I made sure he understood that she wasn't happy with the situation, even if we were. He assured me again, in his next e-mail that he could "handle" any doubts about his counseling her. He said he'd just spend the first session making friends with her and finding out what her interests were. Again, he said to let him know if I had any issues with teachers, and he'd be happy to handle that, too. We passed a few more e-mails back and forth discussing TBI and the effects it has on someone. Every time Jacob reassured me that he would take care of everything.

So Libby started her sophomore year with a 504 Plan and a counselor. I felt a load had been lifted from my shoulders. I could relax a little and not have to be "Super Mom" as she occasionally and sarcastically called me. Libby could learn to do her own homework again, and I might not have to spend every day, waiting by the phone. Maybe I could actually go to lunch, or the mall, or a movie!

The one sad moment came when Libby came to us and said that it wasn't fair to her foal Mozart. He was being ignored and Libby still wasn't strong enough to work with him. Anything that pulled on her arms still put her neck and back into intense pain. She made the decision to sell him. Within two weeks we

found him a home with girls that loved him as much as Libby
wanted to. It was a hard decision, but another necessary change
to our lives. We were no longer horse people; we were a family
that had changed into advocates of brain injury survivors. We no
longer went to horse shows, but to support groups and workshops.
When stopped in the grocery store we no longer talked with our
"horse friends" about horses. When we met, we talked about
recovery and doctors and school.

Sometimes, I would look out at our one hundred ten foot
horse barn with its twenty stalls and would be swept with an
overwhelming sadness, but I wouldn't allow it to last long. "I
can't dwell on the past," I told myself, as I shook my head and
turned my back to the barn. Instead I would think of what was
expected of me today and tomorrow. I wouldn't allow myself to
think beyond that.

Dave, too, had his own struggles with the farm. For a while
he just simply stopped going out to the barn at all, unless it
was absolutely necessary. Then he finally decided to take down
some of the stalls to make a workshop area, where he could go
to escape. He didn't have a clue what he wanted to build, but
he began preparing the new area in the barn for whatever he
decided he wanted it for later. To an outsider, it probably didn't
make much sense, but to us, it made perfect sense. It gave Dave
something to do besides deal with the every day crisis and roller
coaster of TBI; it prepared him, just a little, for better times.
It gave him hope that his future, too, wouldn't always be this
intense. It was to some extent a cleansing process, out with the
old and in with the new. It didn't matter that he didn't know what
that new was; he was ready for it when it came. He began talking
about letting the other two horses go too, but I wasn't ready. I
still clung, just a little, to the past.

We all progress at our own speed. Libby recovered a little at a
time, sometimes up and sometimes down. Looking back we could
see progress. She didn't want to talk about what she was going
through to anyone, not even me, but would rather pretend that
all was normal and as it should be in her teenage life. Once Dave

decided that the horses were in the past and farming was over, he basically washed his hands of it and was ready to move on. He, too, didn't discuss what we were going through. Instead he talked about way in the future, when we could take a vacation, and wouldn't it be great if we didn't have any animals to worry about?

I struggled every step of the way, feeling out of my element, most of the time, resentful, sometimes, but even I too progressed. I researched everything that didn't make sense to me, took classes, talked about what we were going through and cried when I needed to. If I looked back at day one of Libby's accident to a year later, I could see the changes, some good and some bad. I overheard a Mother at the advocacy classes describe what I was feeling very well one day. "It's a club that no one ever wants to join, but once you're in it, it then becomes a club that has open arms and understanding."

CHAPTER 10

Is it better yet?

Libby started her sophomore year with enthusiasm and energy. She was determined to have this year be the year everything would get better in. She was confident and oh so determined to prove to us and the school that she could do this. During the summer we worked on a few new strategies that could help her become more independent. She was ready to try them out.

Dr. Rogers suggested that Libby get a journal and write everything down that she needed to remember. He held up a pen during one of our sessions and told her that this was now an assistant to her brain. After our visit in July, he said he didn't feel it was necessary to continue seeing Libby every month, but that if we needed him for something just to let him know. I felt slightly abandoned, but Libby was thrilled. She'd never enjoyed that hour on the couch. She was determined to show us she didn't need Dr. Rogers anymore.

She started her school year with an agenda, where she could not only write her assignments down, but keep a list of her classes and times taped to the front of it, so if she got lost, she could just glance at her book and know where she needed to be. On her own, Libby also wrote her locker combination inside the back cover because she still had trouble with numbers staying in her memory. That required some adjusting, as the first few weeks showed us. If Libby was in the hallway and couldn't remember what her next class was, she was supposed to look at her agenda. However, if she couldn't remember what time of day it was or the class she had just left, it didn't really help. We had to include a watch that I would remind her to put on every morning. The agenda was great, but if it was put away in her book bag, Libby would often forget it even existed. Unless she was prompted by a teacher, she usually wouldn't remember to write her assignments down. The phrase "Out of sight, out of mind" was a reality for Libby.

Sharon Johnson suggested offering a class to the school district on TBI, hoping to help the teachers understand, just a little bit, what problems they may have during the school year with Libby's short term memory deficits. The school agreed, but only gave us one period in the school day and only offered it to Libby's current teachers. About half of the teachers came. They sat in silence while Sharon presented a power point presentation. I gave them a couple of clues as to what to expect, in regard to forgetting to turn in homework, and the fact that Libby had a tendency to keep repeating a question until she felt comfortable with the answer. I warned them that it could get annoying and may tend to take up class time. She didn't yet comprehend that the class needed to keep rolling along. I got quite a few doubtful looks, but no questions. Most of the teachers carried the attitude that this had been a waste of their free period.

I had met her Global II teacher during our CSE meeting and had talked with him about what to expect. He'd e-mailed me, stating that he had a class that he hadn't been able to get a sub for. He wouldn't be able to attend the TBI class, but would like to talk to me, so I called him. He said that he, too, was a parent of a child with a disability and that he'd do his best to follow the guidelines in her 504 Plan. It was encouraging to know that at least one teacher was willing to do what it took to see Libby succeed.

Her routine quickly became established. Libby seemed so much more receptive to having new teachers and classes than I'd expected. Her energy level stayed high through the first five weeks of school. I'd only been informed about a few missing homework's. She was trying hard to remember to write in her agenda, but was still finding that, if she put it away in her book bag, she'd forget to use it or even remember that she had one

Libby had also made a big decision about her music. She decided that playing in the youth orchestra, at the same time as trying to keep up with her studies was just too much. Actually it was exhausting for her. Almost every time she finished a practice, she would have a migraine. She'd have to go into her bedroom, close all the draperies and sleep. She'd been torn between her love of music and the exhaustion she was feeling and fatigue won. So we no longer made the drive every Sunday afternoon. The result of that was that once her violin teacher was informed that Libby wouldn't be playing in the orchestra; she dropped Libby as a student. Harsh, yes, but just another person who didn't really understand what TBI fatigue can do. We did find another teacher and Libby liked him immediately. She was adamant that she continue with her lessons and since this one thing, playing violin, had been that steady thing that connected her present to her past, we all clung to that and supported Libby any way we could..

Though we thought youth orchestra was over, within the first couple weeks of school, the music director of our local college made an appearance in Libby's class. She invited any interested student to join their youth orchestra. After the first session of youth orchestra, Dr. Alfred invited Libby to participate in the college orchestra, too. Libby was thrilled. I was proud, but concerned that it would be too much for her. After a week of begging and pleading with Dave and me, Libby won out. Now she participated in not just one orchestra, but two, with three practices a week. Thank God the college was only a few minutes away.

Libby learned at the end of 9th grade, that her favorite teacher, Mr. Michaels, had been let go by the school. A new teacher had taken his place. Mr. Michaels had left a tremendous impression on Libby. He'd encouraged her, when she was at her lowest and wanted to give up. He never mentioned her struggles, when some days she just couldn't make her fingers work, but patiently sat with her. He played music for her, when she'd come to him with an emotional meltdown, or just left her alone, when she needed the quiet.

When Libby had reached her point of *"No more"* in 9th grade, she would hide in the practice rooms. I now know that it was because the practice rooms were sound proof. It was a place to go for absolute quiet, which her brain desperately needed, to be able to settle down and come back to a normal thought processes. The school nurse would usually scold her for not coming to the nurse's office. Libby would shrug it off and go to the practice room again and again. Whether the school approved or not, she found her safe place. She cried for weeks, when she found he wouldn't be there for the rest of her high school years.

Now with a new teacher in orchestra, Libby wasn't sure what she was going to do when she needed that quiet time. The school insisted she use either the guidance office or the nurse's office this year. Libby agreed, though she said to me later. "I won't go. They don't get it. It's too noisy and I can still hear the sounds in the hall and people talking."

I decided to just let it play out and see. There was no point in arguing with her, because I actually agreed with her. The school was adamant that she be some place where someone, other than a teacher, could watch over her. It turned out that whenever Libby felt overwhelmed in 10th grade, she'd just call home and refuse to stay at school. I continued to pick her up, when I thought she was really done for the day.

I wish I'd understood this injury better, while we went through these trying times. I know now, that Libby doesn't call, unless she's really done mentally and physically. TBI fatigue is HUGE and can interfere with every aspect of life. The only solution is rest, with absolute quiet. If I had known how important this was, I'd have insisted on a set rest time every day, where she could just go and be quiet. I guess, if I didn't understand it yet, I really couldn't expect the school to, either. Part of our routine became, when it was too much, I'd still come and get her, regardless of the time of day.

Libby seemed better at controlling her emotions, with fewer and fewer meltdowns. It still raised its ugly head once in a while, but her emotional storms went from happening almost every time she got confused or overwhelmed, to once a week, and finally, to once every few weeks. I began to believe, by October, that she was really getting better.

She seemed to be holding her own between school work and orchestra after school. She now had her weekends free. Libby would spend most of the time sleeping trying to regain her strength rather than going to the mall, hanging out with friends, or practicing violin. She didn't complain. Once she'd rested, she did as much homework as she could on Sundays.

By November, Dr. Alfred had actually asked to teach Libby. She insisted that, with all the new music she was learning between the two orchestra's, Dr. Alfred could help her better than her current violin teacher. We agreed. It actually worked really well. Dr. Alfred would teach Libby an hour before orchestra practice, saving us another day of driving. She had just the right amount of compassion and push. She seemed to know instinctively when to back off and when to demand more.

Those first couple months of Libby's sophomore year, we really had high hopes that she would be able to do everything on her own again. Homework, tests, studying, and remembering. Dave and I were thrilled.

One of the worst things we could do was think that traumatic brain injury just goes away. It doesn't. Every time we'd think that things were better, something would happen and shatter our hopes. That is just the way TBI is. You can hope and plan and dream, but you can't make the healing process speed up any faster than the brain is ready to heal. You can get signs of hope one day and have them be dashed the next. My biggest downfall was I refused to accept that fact. I'd grab on to the positives and try to ignore the negatives. I'd be thrilled that Libby didn't call me for two days about anything at school. I convinced myself that, finally that part was over, only to have her call me three times in one day, the minute I'd let my guard down. Healing from a brain injury is like nothing else I can describe.

Healing from a broken bone comes in a natural order. Pain, setting, casting, many weeks and yes sometimes months in a cast and then removal of the cast, maybe a little physical therapy to get the muscle tone back. Yes someday you can probably look forward to arthritis in that area, but, over all, once the bone heals the problem is solved.

Healing from a brain injury is like a roller coaster that doesn't have an end. One day you're up and the next, down. One day the brain cooperates and acts normally and the next it comes to a screeching halt, refusing to perform anything beyond breathing and sleeping. One day the sunshine feels wonderful and the next, looking at the sun causes a blinding migraine. One day you can laugh and the next, even smiling seems impossible. One day you can remember everything and the next, recalling even your own name can seem daunting. Some days the fog is gone and other days, it's so thick you can't see through it or hear anything beyond the beating of your own heart. The worst part of the recovery is that it can last a couple days or a couple years. Only time will tell.

That first night in the hospital, after Libby's accident, did not prepare us for a journey that we'd still be traveling on, an entire year later. When a doctor tells you to wait a couple days, you do. When they say wait a couple weeks, again you do, usually without too much question. If that doctor had said to us, "Wait a year or two" I don't think we could have imagined what that would entail. Our family would have fallen apart. If that same doctor had said that, during that year, we would have to find our own way through this injury because there just isn't anything out there to help families that go through a mild TBI. I don't know what we would have done. Instead, we absorbed what our own brains would allow us to and once Dr. Rogers began telling us "months", even that was so overwhelming; we just didn't know what to do. I think the doctors are right in giving us only the information we can absorb at the time. Even a healthy brain can only absorb so much information, before it, too, becomes overwhelmed.

Libby was now past the point where people expected her to heal any more. Dr. Rogers was so right. That first six months, she had improved rapidly, even though it felt like a snail's pace at the time. The next six months, we could see improvements in the way we handled things, but not so much of a recovery of the injury itself. We were now into the second year and still, just had to wait and see.

Some people we knew seemed tired of the whole Libby thing. Shouldn't she be better? It was just a concussion! We even had a few roll their eyes in disbelief, when they would ask Dave and me how Libby was after not seeing us in months, only to find out that not that much had changed for us. This is where "The Invisible Injury" really comes into play. When time passes, people forget. They forget, unless there is a physical reminder. It's human nature to assume things are better now, even when it isn't.

Over a year after Libby's accident, we thought she remembered everyone again.

A cousin of mine, we hadn't seen since Libby was nine, came back into the state to visit. Libby had absolutely no recall of my cousin. She remembered his son, vaguely remembered where they lived, but looking at my cousin who hadn't changed a bit in all that time...Libby just didn't know him.

For the non-believers or the doubters, I forced myself to smile and walk away. I could continue explaining forever, but either they got it or they didn't. I finally stopped trying and just ignored them. I learned to watch faces. If they really cared, it showed in their face. Those that didn't rolled their eyes and were now a waste of my time. I wasn't even angry at them; I just finally reached the point where there were more important things in life than making all the doubting Thomas's see the light. I now understood the look that I saw on the faces of mothers while shopping with children who had a disability. They watched the faces of the people who didn't understand. The look in their eyes was a direct response to the actions of others.

I think the biggest problem in having others have compassion about an injury is if they can't see the injury, then it just must not be there. TBI and MTBI are the signature injuries in the war in Iraq. That means that thousands and thousands of our sons, daughters, friends, husbands and wives are coming home with this very injury. Some you can see, and some MTBI's are percussion injuries from IED's exploding, not close enough to cause outward physical injuries, but mild traumatic brain injuries caused by the percussion of the blast. Some of our soldiers were misdiagnosed at first as having PTSD, but continued to have problems after the post traumatic stress should have subsided.

Research is now being done which shows that what was once diagnosed as PTSD is actually a traumatic brain injury, in some cases. Finally, organizations like the Brain Injury Association and the Bob Woodruff Foundation are making a difference and bringing awareness to this invisible injury. New technology is now being offered to people that even two years ago didn't exist. Because of the insurgence of men and women suffering brain injuries in the past few years, research and treatment are now in the forefront.

CHAPTER 11

The TBI roller coaster

Five week reports came, and for the first time in a year, I had high hopes that Libby's grades would start improving. I didn't expect them to be where they were before her accident, but, at least, where I could let out that deep breath I'd been holding. Her grades weren't failing, but were in the low to mid seventies again, except for orchestra and choir, which were high nineties. What surprised me were the teacher's comments. She either got *"Libby is a pleasure to have in class"* or *"Work not done, incomplete or late."*

Knowing that it had been an issue last year, I contacted Jacob and asked him to check it out. He got back with me within a couple days and said that Libby was missing homework in almost all of her classes. I asked him if he could please reinforce to the teachers that they needed to remind Libby, daily, to write her assignments down and to remind her to turn her homework in. I assured him that I was double checking and still helping with what homework I saw in her agenda. He assured me he would.

By late November, I began to notice that Libby's migraines were increasing to almost three or four a week. She still had what she called a pressure headache, almost all the time. Her neurologist prescribed two other meds that Libby kept at school that helped, once she got a migraine. I reminded the school nurse and Jacob that at the first sign of headaches, Libby needed to go to the nurse and take her meds. If she waited, they didn't work. She had to catch it at early onset. The teachers were cooperative, but by Christmas break, I heard Libby complain several times that when she went to the nurse, the door was locked and nobody else could get her meds for her. I questioned Jacob and he said he'd look into it. I didn't hear Libby complain about it again, so I assumed he'd done his job and taken care of the matter.

Jacob managed to get one counseling session in with Libby. He e-mailed me, stating she wasn't very cooperative, but he was determined to give it another try. When I asked Libby about it, she said that every time he set a session up it was always during a core class.

"Why can't he just have a session during a study hall so I don't miss class? I get really messed up if I miss one because then I don't know what work has to be done."

When I asked her about her first session, Libby's comment was a very firm. "I told you I didn't like him. I don't want to talk about it," and she wouldn't. I had no idea what took place only that Libby didn't appreciate what he said. I got nothing from Jacob with him explaining it was "counselor, student privacy". He wanted to establish that with Libby. I respected that and didn't press the issue any further.

First report card was a repeat of the five week report. Both comments still played a prominent role in each subject and Libby's grades were again low but passing. The next five week report was very much like the first, but with a few more warning signs. Her grades were slipping. Again I contacted Jacob. This time I asked him if he felt it was necessary or might even be helpful, if we held a parent/teacher conference with all her teachers. He agreed and set one up. Libby, Jacob and I attended, along with three of Libby's teachers. We discussed some options and possible strategies that the teachers could use to keep her focused. Libby's Global teacher suggested some signals, such as tapping the blackboard where the assignments were written down daily, after getting her attention.

One of Libby's big concerns was that she not be the center of attention during class. She was embarrassed that she couldn't remember and didn't want to bring any further attention to herself. There were a few students that began calling her derogatory names or mimic her when she became insistent that a teacher explain what he was trying to say for about the tenth time. Some of the students were becoming impatient with her persistence and the teachers pointed that out to me.

I could only repeat what I'd told them at the TBI class Sharon and I had held. This was a real issue, not just laziness. Libby worked hard on her homework often spending hours on what should have taken her a half hour to complete. She still wasn't reading up to grade level. She had a very hard time comprehending any work that was worded in DBQ (data based questions).

She was, however, doing well in English. I absolutely loved her teacher. A big husky guy who got the kids involved by having them act out whichever book they were reading. Libby responded well to that. She seemed to be able to retain more information in his class than any other. For a ten week homework assignment, she made a 3-D island for the book *"Lord of the Flies."* She was so excited to make this that I took her to the craft store where she found paper that looked like the ocean, sand, grass and rocks. She found tiny fake trees, Spanish moss and decorated the island just as she pictured it from the novel. She got high honor marks. Libby was so proud when her English teacher asked to keep it to show other students what a really good grade looks like. She was thrilled. Libby finally excelled in something other than music.

I could drive myself crazy, wondering how she could be doing so well in one class, but almost failing others because she couldn't understand the subject. It was simple really. The "hands on" teachers did well with Libby and the others struggled. Her

English teacher didn't care if her work was a couple of days late. He never pressured her about it, but just quietly reminded her that she hadn't turned something in. Of course he was the teacher with the comment, "Libby is a pleasure to have in class." The other teachers ranged from doing OK to really having difficulty understanding that they HAD to remind her daily. Often I'd hear from them, "I get so busy, that some days I just don't think to do it," and my response was, "Then you shouldn't penalize Libby for it."

I found that some teachers had a difficult time understanding that Libby's 504 Plan meant she could be late "within reason" with her homework assignments. She could have extended time on her tests. They needed to be responsible for reminding her of any work that needed to be done or turned in. What it boiled down to, in the end, was that some really tried to follow the 504 Plan and others couldn't be bothered.

Libby's Math teacher couldn't be bothered. Thankfully, Libby only had her until the end of second marking period. It didn't seem to matter what Jacob said, what I said, or Libby did. This teacher just didn't really care. If Libby passed the Regents in January, fine. If she didn't, oh, well. I resigned myself that this was just another teacher that we'd have to do our best to stay on her good side and muddle through. I hadn't learned, yet, that you don't have to settle for this poor attitude in teachers. I hadn't learned, yet, that there were things that I could have done, as a parent, to put a stop to this. Libby did pass her regents in the end and we were done with this teacher. I found out later that this teacher and the Biology teacher were very good friends. A representative from the school casually mentioned one day, "If you have trouble with one you have trouble with both."

I was surprised that, later in the year, I was contacted by this very teacher, asking to speak with me. I agreed, not really knowing what she had to say, but met her after school one day.

"Mrs. Parker, I wanted to show you something." She reached for her cell phone. I had no idea where this was leading until I looked down at a picture of a young man, in a hospital bed, with tubes coming out of what seemed everywhere and a bandage on the side of his head. I glanced at this teacher I'd grown to dislike immensely and saw tears in her eyes.

"This is my nephew," she said, her chin trembling. "This was taken at Christmas." Her eyes brimmed with tears and pain. I didn't know what to say to her. Here was obviously a young man with extensive head trauma. I just nodded my head encouraging her to continue.

"I-I just wanted to thank you," she said, "and to say to you I'm sorry. I just didn't understand. I didn't understand."

She bowed her head. I placed my hand on her arm. "Thank you for that. It means so much to hear that," I said quietly. How quickly an enemy can become an ally. "How is your nephew doing now?" I asked.

"Oh, he's improving so much. Soon he'll be home." she said, now smiling. Then a glimmer of sadness passed through her eyes. "He has a long way to go, though."

Again I nodded my head, but before I could say anything, she quickly said. "After he was hurt, I just kept thinking about the class that you and that other woman taught. I just wanted you to know how helpful that is to me now."

I smiled at her and said. "I wasn't sure if anybody was even listening, but thank you for that, too. It's made me feel that it was worthwhile."

I left her classroom feeling light as a feather. This is worth every battle, I thought to myself.

It can get so discouraging, living with someone who has TBI. One day you feel normal; that life is back on that level playing field. Then something happens and knocks you down again, leaving you wondering how you could have ever felt that normal was ever attainable.

Just as I was beginning to doubt that some teachers would ever understand, along comes one I'd given up hope that she'd ever break that cool, uncaring demeanor and she asked for forgiveness. I hated, though, that it took something like her nephews' own injury, for her to see the light. Then again I'm an optimist at heart, so just maybe Libby was put in her path to prepare her for what she'd now be living with in her own family.

Somehow I was becoming an advocate for brain injury. I'd found a goal to look beyond what was happening to us every day. If we could somehow use this to educate others, just maybe, what Libby was going through would have meaning. My advocacy classes were paying off. I'd finished them with a renewed determination to keep fighting and not let ignorance stop Libby from meeting her goals.

She was still determined to graduate with a Regent's diploma, even though her grades were border line. We were still having issues that to me shouldn't have been issues. Instructions were clearly written for the teachers and if Libby was holding up her end, then they should be too. Jacob was helping some, but at times I was beginning to feel the need to respond to the teachers personally.

I began to make sure that along with the problems, I acknowledged the successes with each individual teacher. I knew what a struggle the teachers had keeping everything in order for Libby. I had been a thorn in their sides off and on last year, and my classes taught me that acknowledging even the small successes was important to the teachers too.

Libby was still having difficulty writing. If she made a mistake, which was often, I'd sometimes find her tearing up her paper and starting again. On ditto's, she'd make a mess and be so upset at the way the paper looked; she wouldn't want to hand it in. It was almost becoming obsessive-compulsive, with her, to have a neat paper. It would sometimes take her over an hour to write just a short essay because she'd start over, again and again.

After school one day, she said to me. "I need wite-out. Can we go to Wal-Mart and get some?"

I was tired and had just started dinner. "Can it wait until I go shopping tomorrow? I'm in the middle of fixing dinner." Plus, it didn't help that the nearest Wal-Mart was over a half hour away.

"No, Mom, I need it now." Libby was insistent.

She had reached a point in her recovery where everything had to be spoken now or done now. If she didn't say it or do it immediately, later it might be gone from her memory. It was irritating but understandable.

"Libby what if I write it on my grocery list and I promise to get it tomorrow," I said, hoping to appease her.

"No, MOM, we have to get it tonight."

"Why!"

"Because my teacher and I figured something out and I need it to do my homework." She began to explain that over the past week, her English teacher had seen her tearing up her papers too. He simply set a bottle of wite-out on her desk and told her to try that instead. It worked. That simple suggestion had cut her writing time down by half, just because she no longer had to write and rewrite entire pages.

After dinner, we went and bought several bottles, plus the white tape for bigger mistakes. I watched my daughter happily complete one assignment after another in record time. After Libby was asleep, I went to my computer and e-mailed her teacher, thanking him for wite-out. I know it sounds silly, but just a simple suggestion can make such a difference sometimes. I wanted this teacher to know that even the little things are appreciated. He responded in good humor, telling me that it had gotten to be quite a joke between Libby and him and that he was glad to help.

For a while after Libby's accident, I wanted someone to blame, someone to take out my frustrations on. I researched everyone who was at the accident scene that could have taken the initiative and called an ambulance. If I thought about it too much, it still bothered me. I'd find myself placing blame out of anger, sometimes warranted, but sometimes it was just as simple as a mother striking out because her child had changed because of someone else's actions. I was now at the point in Libby's recovery where I really wanted to be done with those feelings of anger. I began reaching out, in as positive a way as I could, to any teacher or anyone who was employed at the school.

Libby was improving, even though she still had some major issues and impairments. I watched her. Very seldom did I see her angry because of her accident. She might get upset or frustrated at a teacher or because of her fatigue, but, every once in a while now, we'd see just a little of that bubbly, smiling daughter. Even though we were learning to live with our new normal, we still got glimpses of the old Libby and we'd grab on to those moments, treasuring them, learning, though, that the next day would be different and those times weren't the norm. It didn't stop Dave and me from clinging to them desperately. I was so grateful to anyone who could bring back Libby's smile, if only for a moment. It was what I found I missed the most.

When Libby was a freshman, because of her accident she'd missed picture day which was usually taken a few weeks after school starts. Instead we took Libby to Wal-Mart and had them take her freshman picture. In that picture, it showed very little of what Libby was going through. She sat up properly and smiled for the camera. Anyone that glanced at that picture would never know the seriousness of what she was going through. Looking deeper at the picture, I could see that the smile didn't reach her eyes. They were dull and not sparkling the way they used to be. I could also see that no lighting could change the pallor of her skin. She was white. Libby's natural color in September is a deep tan from spending her entire summer outside with the horses.

In Libby's sophomore year, her pictures were taken at school. When I got them I was thrilled. She had a genuine smile; her eyes held that little sparkle and her color was so much better. I didn't let myself think that it had obviously been a good day for Libby, but put that picture on the wall, just below the one that had been taken just about a month after her accident. I refuse to take that picture down only because comparing it to her most recent pictures reminds me how far she's come in her recovery.

A clue to whether Libby would start her day as a good day or bad day was the way she dressed for school. If she came out of her room, with her hair styled, makeup on and in her favorite clothes, it was going to be a good day. If she came out with no makeup, her hair down, barely brushed and just any old t-shirt, I stayed out of her way, but carefully would go through our morning ritual.

"Do you have your watch on? Do you have your agenda? Did you brush your teeth? Do you have all your homework?" Normally, I'd ask those questions every morning with other's thrown in, depending on what I knew would be expected of her that particular day. Usually Libby would give answers in the affirmative or I'd hear "Oops," and she'd run back into her bedroom for something she'd forgotten. On her bad days, I would just get a grunt from her. Very seldom did she respond beyond that. Once she walked down the drive to get on the bus, I'd let out that breath I'd been holding all morning, in expectation of a possible meltdown even before school started.

CHAPTER 12

Betrayal

In February of 2008, we had our second session of depositions. Our attorneys came to the school this time and interviewed Kelly, Libby's tutor, and the school nurse, that attended to the injured students on Libby's bus, directly after the accident. They also wanted to talk to Jacob and Fred Simmons, the bus superintendent. I was the only one in our family to attend this meeting.

Frank, our attorney, brought what I thought was an assistant with him. A tiny, power ball named Cheryl. He informed me that he wanted Cheryl on Libby's case. Frank said that when they presented in front of a jury it was much easier for the jury to hear about female issues and emotions from another woman than from a male attorney. He took me aside and assured me that Cheryl was a wonderful attorney and he had very good reasons for bringing her in on our case. I let him know that I'd be agreeable to having her on the team, but that it might take a while to trust that this was in Libby's best interest.

I had visions of Frank growing tired of the case, or just possibly it wasn't important to him anymore, so he was sloughing us off to one of his younger, less experienced attorneys. I'd noticed that, more and more, his paralegal, Denise, would call instead of Frank, but really I knew nothing about what attorneys do and could only guess. In reality, Denise did a great job. She and I formed a nice working relationship. I agreed to give Cheryl a go, mainly because I hadn't been given me much of a choice. Frank just brought her. If we were to present a united front at the school, I'd just have to play along.

They started by having Libby's bus brought out front and they all filed on the bus, taking pictures of the very last seat on the passenger side where she'd been sitting when the bus had been rear-ended. As I walked with the attorneys, the bus superintendent and principal, I felt tears welling up and my throat choking with emotion. It was a cold blustery day, but in spite of the cold, I could feel my palms sweating and my heart pounding. Here, all this time, I'd considered myself a strong woman capable of handling anything that was thrown at me and now I couldn't walk up those few steps and get on that bus. As everyone else filed up the steps, I froze.

"Stop this!" I thought to myself. "Don't fall apart now."

I finally managed to take two steps onto the bus, but that was it. I felt foolish, hoping no one would notice. I had presented the façade of a strong person to the school, lawyers and anyone else connected with Libby's accident. I just couldn't start blubbering like a baby now. I had to pull myself together and carry on and I did.

The first person deposed was Fred. He truly surprised me. He admitted to feeling he'd made mistakes about the accident. He acknowledged anything that Cheryl brought up that would make him accountable. I admired him for stepping up and being honest. It didn't, however, make the school attorney happy.

Then it was Kelly's turn. As she sat, she gave me a big smile. Though obviously nervous, Kelly seemed willing to answer questions. I hadn't seen her in almost a year. It was still nice to see Kelly, even under these circumstances.

She was a trouper and was actually a great help to the case. Because she'd taught Libby before her accident, then spent over four months tutoring her after the accident, she presented a very clear picture of who our daughter used to be and what she'd become since her TBI. At one point, I noticed Kelly actually made a point of being qualified to teach. She also stated, very clearly, how easy Libby had been to teach in 6th grade and how hard it was after her accident. She was adamant that, through it all, Libby was still a joy to teach, even through the most difficult days. She surprised me when, at one point, Kelly became insistent that she was qualified to answer any questions our attorneys may want to ask. It immediately took me back to the parent/teacher conference experience we'd shared. I was pretty sure that was what she was referring too.

What I found out a few weeks later was that the school attorney had tried to encourage Kelly to answer questions with "Oh, I'm sorry. I'm not qualified to answer that." He pressed her several times that, if she felt at all out of her element, she should respond with that statement. He angered Kelly so much because he'd talked down to her. She made sure that he and the school both understood she felt very qualified to answer any questions.

It was then the nurses' turn in the hot seat. Cheryl asked her many questions about the accident scene, what it was like on the bus, and how she came to realize that Libby was injured. The nurse stated that she didn't think Libby had been injured, even though Libby had raised her hand when she asked if anyone was hurt. Her reasons were that Libby responded to her questions. When Cheryl asked her what questions she had asked Libby, the nurse responded. "Well, I asked her if she was hurt and she said yes. I asked her where she hurt and she said my head, neck and back. I figured that, since she'd answered my questions, she wasn't in any serious danger."

The nurse was looking confident and sure of her answers not even understanding just how ludicrous her statement sounded. When Cheryl asked if she heard Libby tell how old she was, the nurse responded that she'd heard her tell the trooper her age. Cheryl then asked the nurse if she actually knew how old Libby was.

"No, I guess I don't," the nurse responded, looking just a little uncomfortable.

The longer this woman talked, the more convinced I was that she was NOT qualified. Yes, she was an RN, but it appeared she had little knowledge of what to do or how to treat someone with a head trauma. She admitted not really being able to see Libby's eyes because she hadn't brought a flashlight and "yes" Libby's eyes were very dark, and "yes" she had a hard time seeing her pupils, but she just did her best.

Cheryl then asked her a question that surprised me. "How many injury reports did you and the other nurse fill out between the two busses?"

Her answer was, "Thirteen". I'd had no idea that many students had been injured. Up until that point, I'd only known about the seven who were at the ER when I had taken Libby the first time.

"So, you're telling me that even though you filled out thirteen injury reports, you didn't feel it was necessary to call for an ambulance?" Cheryl asked.

"Well, no, I didn't think any of them were serious enough. It took the other nurse and me twenty four hours to get all the injury reports written up. We didn't even finish them until the next day at school, but as for an ambulance being called? I discussed it with Mrs. Crabner. We decided, together, that we had everything under control." The nurse shifted nervously in her chair.

"So tell me again then, how did you determine that Libby didn't have any serious injury?"

The nurse told how she'd questioned Libby again, asked her to squeeze her fingers and looked into her eyes. She didn't have a flashlight so she really couldn't see that well. She had parted Libby's hair and looked at the back of her head. When she found no blood, she determined that Libby was not in danger and continued on to the next student.

"Can I ask you then," Cheryl continued. "What does a closed head injury look like?"

"Objection," The schools' attorney interjected.

"Withdraw the question." Cheryl stated, smiling directly at the attorney.

It was then Jacob's turn. I quickly learned that Cheryl WAS the right woman for our team. She began by questioning him on his honesty. Was he honest every time he talked with me or Libby? His response was a definite "Yes". Was he honest in all of his e-mails? "Yes." Cheryl continued asking him about his honesty until he became red faced and I could see he was getting angry.

I quickly jotted a note to Frank and reminded him that Jacob was the only person in this school district who was helping us. I was starting to worry that Cheryl would upset the apple cart and we'd be left with no one again.

Cheryl asked to go off the record and speak with me privately and took me outside the door. "Naomi, I'm going to ask you to trust me here. I have certain information that Jacob is not who he presents himself to be to you," she said firmly.

"But he's the only one who's helping us," I said grasping for that last little hope that she might be wrong.

"Just trust me and see where this goes. You'll understand in a few minutes. I promise." The seriousness in Cheryl's face convinced me, so I agreed. We walked back into the room and sat down.

Immediately Cheryl went back on the record and continued. "OK, Jacob, now that we have established that you're an honorable person, let me ask you. Do you believe that Libby has a traumatic brain injury?"

"Objection! He's not qualified to answer that." The opposing attorney said hotly.

"Let me rephrase my question then. Did you ever tell anyone employed at this school that you didn't believe that Libby had a traumatic brain injury?"

"Objection!" This time the opposing attorney stood up." You can't ask him that!"

"Yes, I can, I'm simply asking him a question about a conversation that he may or may not have had." Cheryl remained seated, but her pretty blue eyes had turned the color of steel.

"If you're going to persist with this type of questioning, I'm going to call for the judge. You can't ask him these questions. I won't allow it."

"By all means, call for a judge. Let me remind you, however, it's a Friday afternoon and you'll be the one messing with his weekend plans, not me."

The attorney sat back down, and an off the record discussion took place. Both sides discussed whether a judge needed to be present. It was finally decided if Cheryl asked a question that the school attorney objected to, he would announce objection, but would then instruct Jacob to answer, giving the judge an opportunity, later, to have the conversation withdrawn from the deposition. I had no idea they could even do that.

When they went back on the record, Cheryl pulled out Libby's neuropsych test that the school had used to form her 504 Plan and asked Jacob to read through it and point out anything that he didn't agree with.

Another explosive objection was heard, and another off the record discussion took place about Jacob's qualifications and again, Cheryl got her way.

Once Jacob began speaking, it became very clear what Cheryl had been trying to tell me. From the beginning, he didn't believe that Libby had a TBI, and had openly questioned the school district about the validity of Dr. Roger's testing. He felt that Libby may have an underlying mental disorder. He didn't agree that the accident had caused her deficits. He again brought up the lawsuit and used it as an excuse as to why he hadn't brought his real feelings to my attention, but had played along with us. He stated that the school felt that I was an over-reactive mother out looking for cash and there really wasn't anything all that wrong with Libby. He'd discussed this with administration and they all decided to wait it out until the lawsuit had proved them right before challenging us.

All through Jacob's speech, the school attorney objected, but let him continue. By the end of the deposition I couldn't wait for Cheryl to tear him apart. While he spoke, I never took my eyes off him but glared coldly, hoping just once he'd glance my way. He never did. That sweet, soft spoken man, who swore he would help us and was so understanding about TBI, was an outright liar. He'd been put on our case, not to help us, but to gather any incriminating evidence that would help the school's case and not ours. All those times he e-mailed me compassionately, with understanding, explaining things about TBI and how we might be able to help Libby, was just a way to get more information against us. He never believed that Libby was injured and made it sound like she had problems in her past that would account for what was happening today. He even questioned the fact that Libby hadn't remembered her emergency room doctor the night of the accident.

Jacob never got the opportunity to counsel Libby that second time. When I went home that evening, Libby's response was. "See I told you I didn't trust him." She was right and I told her so. I apologized for pushing him on to her and promised I'd trust her judgment in the future.

Then she opened up and told Dave and me about that first counseling session. He'd actually never mentioned TBI to her at all, but asked her if her father or mother abused her physically or sexually. He then asked her if her mom and dad fought a lot and if so, did they ever get physical? Libby had answered a firm "No" to each question and finally asked him, "What does this have to do with TBI? This is crap I'm going back to Global!" She got up and left his office, without another word exchanged between them. No wonder he didn't want to tell me about their session.

That was the day I stopped being naïve and began to pay attention to Libby's reactions more. She may not understand conversations sometimes and mix up the meaning of something when someone was sarcastic to her, but she still trusted her gut. Now I did too. It was a lesson learned for me and a crushing blow for my hopes in dealing with the school. If they'd done this, how could I trust anyone employed there? How could I know if they were really concerned about Libby's successes, or just pacifying that over-reactive mother?

Jacob was never present again at any teacher meeting, nor did we exchange even a single e-mail between us. He was quietly removed from Libby's 504 Plan the following year. We've never discussed him or what happened that day with anyone at the school. I went back to e-mailing teachers with my concerns. I'd even stopped asking Mr. King for help. Instead I went directly to Sandy, the CSE chairperson. Never again did I forget that the school was playing along until our lawsuit was finished. Was it because the insurance company's attorney told them to? I was never sure about that. On occasion I would feel genuine concern from a teacher or Mr. King. I accepted that for what it was, but could never quite get it out of my head that they, too, could just be playing along, biding their time.

I was so angry at this betrayal. I had, from every step of the way, been obnoxiously open about Libby's impairments, to everyone at the school. I was so determined to make them understand what did and didn't work in class, what helped Libby remember and what didn't, what they, as teachers, needed to do in the case of a meltdown that I never expected that they would actually not believe that she even had a brain injury.

Were we doing the right thing by pursuing this lawsuit? Was it what was stopping the school from just seeing what was in front of their faces? Do we drop it, in hopes that if we did, they would believe us? Doubts crept into my thoughts, but even as I questioned myself about doing the right thing, I knew the answer. Yes it was the right thing. My daughter had suffered for over a year and a half with TBI. It didn't matter that her medical scans showed nothing. We knew, her doctors knew, and underneath it all, I knew that the school knew, too. What happened with Jacob was definitely a result of the lawsuit, but it didn't change anything else. Libby used to be able to do Math and languages and read at often five grade levels above her current grade. It all showed in her standardized testing. Now she couldn't do them.

Libby lost any chance at academic scholarships because of what she'd gone through. Her lawsuit would compensate for that, if nothing else. She was still determined to go to college. We definitely didn't have the luxury of just paying for her college. Libby understood all along, that if she wanted something bad enough, she'd have to work hard to attain what she wanted. What Libby wanted was a minimum of four years of college to become a music teacher, or music therapist. Since going through all of her therapy and understanding how much music helped her, Libby was now leaning toward music therapy. Regardless, music played a big role in Libby's future.

If the school wanted to believe that I was a money hungry parent, out looking for a handout then let them. I knew the truth and I now understood that if we lost this lawsuit, the school would have every excuse ready to pull any accommodations we had fought so hard to get for Libby. There was no way we could let this drop now. We had to see this through to the end.

What is wrong with this world that a parent is put in this position; that I would have to prove my daughter was really hurt? Couldn't they understand what we were going through every day? Couldn't they see the changes that had happened within our family and in Libby's life alone? Maybe they couldn't see what happened within our family, but they could see the difficulty Libby still had in school, even after a year and a half. They could still see that every time she participated in Phys-Ed and became active enough to raise her pulse, she'd have to go the nurse for her meds. I know they could see the physical changes in Libby. She'd gained forty pounds since her accident, from being so sedentary, and the medications she now had to remember to take twice a day.

I was swept back to that angry place I'd tried so hard to avoid. This just isn't real, this only happens in the movies, not our lives. It took me many sleepless nights and exhausting days to get myself back to that calmer place where I could look at things objectively. I needed help, Libby needed help. In reality, our family needed someone to work this out with. There were times when I thought Dave's and my marriage was falling apart. Other times we'd lie in bed at night, not talking, just holding hands, exhausted from all the turmoil. It was time to find counseling for all of us. I remembered, in one of my advocacy classes, a doctor had come for the afternoon with instructions on how to take care of yourself and your family. I got out my notebooks and looked up her number.

CHAPTER 13

Nurse Ratchet

We looked for and found a new counselor who actually worked with Libby on strategies that would take over when her memory failed her. She also worked with her on coping with TBI and encouraged her to advocate for herself. It was everything we'd hoped the school would provide and hadn't. Every Thursday I drove Libby to see her counselor, but once a month they would be available for Dave and me if we needed to talk. Dave, in his usual way, went once and said he was healed. Me? I looked forward to that visit.

We continued our vigilance, when teachers began to complain. Libby wasn't turning in work and every time we asked them if they were reminding her, we heard, "I have so many other students; I can't be expected to remember her every day."

Our response was, "Well, it say's you have to in her 504 Plan."

It was now May of 2008. We'd been dealing with all these issues for more than a year and a half. I kept thinking that, at some point, this will sink in to these teachers that a TBI just doesn't go away. Libby had failed two classes third marking period. She was placed on academic ineligibility, preventing her from going to "Soph Hop," the sophomore formal dance. I was beginning to feel lost again and exhausted from keeping that constant vigil. Sharon suggested that I attend the annual Brain Injury Conference that was being held in Albany. I registered, hoping the workshops would help. They held four workshops daily for two days on coping strategies and information workshops such as "Learnet" a website for students with TBI. I couldn't wait to get there.

The day before I was to go, Libby came home from school and asked me if I thought she was Bi-polar. I answered a definite "No" and asked her why?

"Well, the nurse told me today she thought I was Bi-polar and that I needed to be on medicine for it." She shrugged. "Isn't that what Grandpa has?"

"Yes, honey, it is, and I can assure you, you are not Bi-polar. I lived with Grandpa for twenty years. I know very well what it is and what it can do to a person. Why would the nurse think you have it?"

"Well, she said her son had it and I acted just like him, so I must have it too."

I was livid. How dare the nurse diagnose my daughter? Not only was she not qualified as a nurse to diagnose anyone, but obviously she'd heard nothing I'd said about what TBI can do to a person. Yes, it has some characteristics of Bi-polar Disorder, along with characteristics of Attention Deficit Hyperactive Disorder (ADHD) and Obsessive Compulsive Disorder (OCD), but it was still traumatic brain injury at its finest. I assured Libby that she was not Bi-polar and dropped the subject. I knew that when people offered suggestions to Libby regarding her injury or health, she took everything to heart.

For anyone reading this I in no way want to diminish these diseases. They have their own set of issues and solutions. I understand that each of these disabilities can be crushing to that person and his family but to muddle our already muddy waters and just casually throw out a diagnosis was the last straw.

Libby had started falling down, a few months back; we were trying to figure out why. If the cat ran in front of her, in a completely open room, and it startled Libby, she might fall to the floor. She'd fallen down the stairs at school several times and down the bus steps on two separate occasions, injuring her tailbone both times. Her doctors were working on a solution, but had yet to come up with one. Just another trick up ole TBI's sleeve or another piece of the puzzle to try to solve. Another round of doctor visits, that weren't on her regular schedule, had Libby panicky about her health again.

This time, I was going to squash this before it had a change to become anything but a short conversation. I was at the school, first thing the following morning and went directly to the nurse's office. I asked to speak with her privately, so she took me into a small room inside the nurse's station and shut the door.

"Just what were you thinking when you told Libby you thought she was Bi-polar yesterday?" I looked directly at her face. It registered shock and then a little panic.

"I never told her that," she denied, her eyes not quite looking at me, but bouncing around the room.

"Then why would my daughter come home to me, ask me if she was Bi-polar and tell me that you did?"

"Well, if she did that she lied," she said loudly. "I never told Elizabeth that. I said to her that she was moody and seemed depressed."

"Of course she's depressed," I said hotly. "She's on antidepressants for it. You know that. It's in your record. Look at what she's been going through this last year. Anyone would be depressed."

"She shows the classic symptoms of being Bi-polar. One day she's in here moody and the next, she's singing down the hallway." A look of guilt passed quickly over her face, as she realized that she'd just slipped up and practically confessed to me that she had indeed, said that Libby was Bi-polar.

"Over this past year have you heard or learned anything about traumatic brain injury? Libby has good days. That's when her brain is cooperating. She had bad days and that's when her brain isn't functioning properly. She also has tendencies of OCD and ADHD, but that doesn't mean she has either of those. It's just what a brain injury does to a person. The ADHD comes from the fact that she no longer is able to focus for long periods of time and then fatigue tells her brain to stop. The OCD is because she has to be sure she's done something and her short term memory won't always remember that she has, so she has to make sure. What you said to her was way out of line and very inappropriate. You are not qualified to diagnose my daughter and then tell her what meds she needs to be on." Sarcastically, I said, "Let's leave that to the professionals."

"If you think you're so knowledgeable then I suggest you learn a little more about being Bi-polar. My son is and let me tell you, it's no picnic. In fact, I've moved out of my home because of it." She was determined to prove me wrong.

"And just because your son is my daughter has to be too?" I asked all the while thinking that this woman was just unbelievable. "Let me tell you something! My father went through hell his entire life because he went undiagnosed for Bi-polar Disorder until he was in his forties. I know and understand the disease very well and I don't need you to tell me. It is something I've watched very closely for in all my children. I understand the signs. Until Libby's accident and her TBI, she's never done anything that would make me think she had Bi-polar Disorder." I was on a roll. I wasn't ready to stop talking even though I watched the nurses' mouth open several times in protest, though no words came out.

"I suggest, before you go any further with this conversation you take some time to look up TBI online or get some books and educate yourself. You're Libby's nurse, for God sake. She needs to come here for her meds, but she doesn't have to come in here and listen to this. I have tried every way I can to help this school learn about TBI, but if you don't want to listen or learn, I can't force you. I will tell you this and I'll make it easy for you to understand. You can be part of the problem or you can be part of the solution. It's your choice. And if you ever tell my daughter again that she has anything other than what she has, I'll report you." My voice was clear, but very quiet and I looked coldly into her eyes, seeing fear register on her face. "Oh, and one more thing. Your son isn't Bi-polar. He is your son, just like Libby is my daughter. They just happen to have a disability. They aren't the disability."

Before she had time to respond, I walked out of her office and out the door of the school, got in my car and drove the three hour trip to Albany. I think my hands quit shaking when I got to Binghamton.

I attended all the workshops I could squeeze in. I saw Sharon once in a while, but for the most part, I was on my own. It was at that conference that I met hundreds of people that had a TBI. By the end of the first day, I realized something important. All along I'd been at odds, telling myself that Libby wasn't seriously injured because it would have shown up on scans or her face or something. I also knew that her responses to circumstances, her short term memory problems and amnesia said she was. What I found was that only a minority of the people at the conference showed any outward physical signs of having a brain injury.

Every year 1.4 million people sustain brain injuries. Out of that number approximately 50,000 people die from TBI. 235,000 people are considered serious enough to stay in the hospital to go through some type of therapy to regain some of what they've lost in speech, motor function, or other cognitive impairment. Sometimes these people may or may not have that outward physical appearance that shows the rest of the world that they indeed have a TBI. 1,100,000 people are treated and released from the emergency room, some without even a TBI diagnosis, every year with no rehabilitation or counseling provided. They are basically left to fend for themselves waiting for their concussion to go away.

For the first time, I met people very much like Libby. No physical sign showing everyone else that they had a TBI, but they were there at the conference, just like I was. I wished I'd brought Libby so she could see she wasn't alone, but she'd had so many absences already, I didn't want to make getting through the school year even harder for her.

Over and over, I heard throughout the day "Are you a TBI survivor or caregiver?" I couldn't tell. I found myself asking the same question when seated at the large round dining tables. What an eye opener, to see so many people suffering the same symptoms as my daughter and not able to tell, unless you asked them outright. It was also that weekend that this book became just a seed of thought; several people said to me that I should write a book about Libby's story and what we were going through.

A TBI survivor has to face the fact, that certain things they used to be able to do, they now have difficulty doing. The memory that they could, is still there, ingrained in their subconscious. He or she spends each day trying so hard just to act normal around others, hiding the inadequacies when they can, trying and trying and trying new methods to help with these newly acquired deficits. All along telling themselves and others they aren't stupid, while those that don't understand think just that.

Many people had faced and conquered exactly what Libby was going through. It had taken some of them decades, sometimes only because of the lack of understanding of mild TBI. These people encouraged me to write her story. Maybe, Libby's story may just help others down the road, and just maybe they wouldn't have to go through all the tribulations that these people did.

I came home, once again rejuvenated, with the thoughts of Nurse Ratchet behind me. I was ready to face whatever might come our way next. I now had some ideas as to why Libby was falling down too. I'd learned, while I was there, that some antidepressants and migraine meds don't work well together and can cause clumsiness. I called the neurologist and she agreed that might be the reason and changed Libby's Periactin to Topomax. Libby stopped falling down.

I'd also grabbed as many information pamphlets from each booth I could get my hands on. Monday, after I returned home, I took them down to the nurse and set them on her desk. "I thought you might like these, they're very educational." She didn't say a word as I turned around and walked out. I'm sure she threw them in the trash before I got to my car, but it made me feel ever so much better. When I got home, I e-mailed each of Libby's teachers, telling them about a website I'd learned about called "Learnet". It's a place for teachers to go when they have a student with a TBI. It actually walks them through several options to help that student become more successful.

I'd made a decision on my way to Albany. I wasn't going to tolerate any more ignorance from the nurse or anyone else at the school, or even outside the school. I'd given them every opportunity to learn about TBI. I'd heard just about enough from Nurse Ratchet. Throughout the year, as I picked Libby up from school because of fatigue, I'd hear her comments of, "You're falling for that? That's just a typical teenage thing." Or "That's so typical all the kids are doing this." Every time she made her comments, I'd held my tongue, but it irked me.

Karen (Nurse Ratchet) didn't understand that Libby liked school. Libby was upset when she had to miss it and this nurse just didn't get it. I'd come to the conclusion that this was just another person on our growing list who probably never would. I had to be so careful to not talk about this in front of Libby, because this was the place she was supposed to go when she had difficulty with her TBI or started a migraine. She still had to come back here and interact with this woman. I couldn't let my anger interfere with that.

So I set my feelings aside, held my tongue, smiled at the nurse when I came to pick Libby up and hoped and prayed that she wouldn't take our argument out on Libby. If she did, that would be it. No more messing around, placating feelings and pretending all was well at the nurse's office.

CHAPTER 14

Knowledge is Power

One of the biggest transformations in my own life was finding that the search for answers gave me an outlet for the anger I often felt. Just when I'd think I had a handle on my anger, some little thing at school would happen and there it was again. I was sure I'd reached that stage where I'd been angry at what happened to Libby, had dealt with it and could look at life calmly again. But throughout our journey with TBI, I learned that anger doesn't get dealt with. It serves a purpose. For me it was always reaching that point of frustration and anger, when it looked like we had come up against a brick wall in Libby's recovery that drove me on to search harder for answers.

The internet is a wonderful tool. If you have the time to sit and look at page after page, or the knowledge to quickly find what you're looking for, which is something I still haven't attained, you can find answers to almost every topic. It's where I went when Dr. Rogers first mentioned "TBI vulnerability". I had no idea what that meant so I Googled it. I found thousands of sites, each with a little different twist on the definition, but in general laymen's terms, its definition means that after a person has acquired a TBI they become vulnerable to other cognitive impairments, such as an inability to control their emotions.

In my search, I found a checklist that I printed out. This checklist asked about four pages of TBI related questions and gave a range of one through four (one, meaning this happens always and four, it never happens). It came in different sections that were related to different fields, emotions, short term memory, and how the patient actually views himself. Libby helped me fill out the checklist when she was about four months post injury. The score scared me to death. We answered a few answers with ones, the majority twos, some threes and even a couple of fours. What became useful in this checklist was, about four months later, we took the test again and could see that some of the ones were now twos, that there were a lot more threes, and even a few more fours.

When you're dealing with TBI, you can't look daily and see the improvements. If you look for those advances every few months you might see a little. By continuing to fill out this checklist every couple of months, Libby could actually see where she was improving. It was so hard for her to see any progress at all that this checklist became a good morale booster.

The Internet was also where I found the Brain Injury Association and was guided to Sharon Johnson. Once I found Sharon, she was the one I went to for information. If I had a question about anything TBI or school related, Sharon had, if not the answer, at least the place to look for the answer. She was always supportive, no matter how small the problem was for Libby. She encouraged me to look at other organizations for support. Sharon gave me the information for Parent to Parent and The Advocacy Center. Sharon suggested I go to the workshop that P2P held. It was there I first began to learn the part 200 Regulations for the Department of Education. It was there I was handed my health care notebook.

Whenever the family has a CSE meeting with a school, the school is supposed to hand out or mail the Part 200 Regulation section regarding parent's rights. I received mine in my notebook from The Advocacy Center along with the rest of the Part 200 Regulations. We were encouraged, in that first workshop, to really study these regulations. That evening I learned 200.4 "Procedures for referral, evaluation, individualized education program (IEP) development, placement and review. In 200.4 I learned that a referral may be made by many different people (i) "a student's parent or person in parental relationship."(ii) "A professional staff member of the school district, in which the student resides, or the public or private school the student legally attends." There are others who can also refer a student for evaluation. Reading this made me wonder why hadn't anyone in Libby's school referred her as soon as they knew she'd been injured or at least referred her when I came to them in October of 2006, telling them that Libby might not recover for months?

In April of 2007 I'd written our principal asking for a meeting for evaluation and referral. I never got a response from the school. In part (4) I learned "If a referral is received by the building administrator, it shall be forwarded to the committee chairperson immediately upon its receipt by the administration." This was either never done, or if it was forwarded, then the committee chairperson dropped the ball and never contacted CSE. Our committee chairperson was none other than Mrs. Crabner, our school superintendent.

Part (9) of that same section reads "The building administrator, upon receipt of a referral or copy of a referral, may request a meeting with the parent or person in parental relationship to the student, and the student, if appropriate, to determine whether the student would benefit from additional general education support services as an alternative to special education, including the provision of educationally related support services, speech and language improvement services, academic intervention services, and any other services designed to address the learning needs of the student and maintain a student's placement in general education with the provision of appropriate educational and support services."

This was never done for Libby. Also in part (9) it reads "A copy of the agreement shall also be placed in the student's cumulative education record file. The meeting: (i) shall be conducted within 10 school days of the building administrator's receipt of the referral" Again, this was never done. I'd written my request for evaluation April 7, 2007 and was now taking this workshop the end of July. I learned so much in that three hour workshop. I learned how to write a proper CSE letter, I learned that the school doesn't have to listen when you say, "My child needs this or that", but they do have to pay attention when you say, "This isn't appropriate for my child's education."

School districts have to provide a Free and Appropriate Public Education (FAPE) under the Individuals with Disabilities Education Act (IDEA) in the Least Restrictive Environment (LRE). Yes, people we are now entering the world of acronyms. The Americans with Disabilities Act of 1990 (ADA), Section 504 of the Rehabilitation Act of 1973 became an important tool to me when carrying on conversations with the members of our school district. For the first time, I learned that a student with a disability has the option of an IEP or a 504 Plan. In basic terms the IEP covers more, is government funded and can follow a student into college. A 504 Plan isn't funded by the government and doesn't necessarily follow that student into college. It's that middle ground between an IEP and general education.

That evening, I also received a health care notebook. Sharon Marrella explained how important this notebook is to parents because there was a section to keep track of medical information, such as lab work done and dates, prescriptions, family information, health care providers, and more. It was a nice organized way to keep everything we'd need when going from Libby's general doctor, to her neurology appointments, to her psychiatry appointment. I soon added my own tweak to the notebook with a school section. I kept Libby's report cards, letters from the school that needed Dr. Rogers or our counselor's attention and all the copies of Libby's file at school.

In August of 2007, I started taking advocacy classes with Jean Tydings at our local library. Every Thursday I'd go from

10:00 a.m. – 2:00 p.m. which allowed me to be home in time for Libby once school started. For eight weeks, I learned so much and met so many other parents sharing the same problems with their school districts. We held mock CSE meetings, based on the experiences of the people in the room and learned how to maneuver through these meetings without feeling overwhelmed. We studied the part 200 Regulations. We learned, in detail, what the differences were between EIP's and 504 Plans.

There, we learned that anger never goes away. As parents, we are allowed to grieve what we lost. I lost my vivacious fourteen-year old, who had bounded into the house every day, jabbering away non-stop, for at least the first fifteen minutes, about the going's on at school. Before the accident she was a teenage ball of energy who was excited about her future, and proms, and boyfriends. In its place, I learned to love the now fifteen-year old who rarely smiled when she got off the bus. She hardly ever talked about school unless it also included tears and frustration and had stopped bounding anywhere. She now walked at a much slower pace. Boys were never talked about and were, at this point in her recovery, I think, rarely thought about because Libby was just too wrapped up in relearning and remembering to do much else.

Whether we as parents want to acknowledge it or not, emotions play a big part in our decision making. Just learning that it was OK to be angry and grieve, made such a difference in the way I handled the every day things.

Knowing this somehow made the anger, grief, frustration and all those other negative emotions not as powerful anymore. They were real, but I could learn to use them in a positive way if I chose. When I got angry, I began looking for answers, when I became frustrated over someone's ignorance, I began educating. When I grieved, I now gave myself permission to cry and be sad and I found in doing that I came out the other side feeling stronger. I could appreciate and learn to love who my daughter was becoming but it was still OK to grieve for that part of the child I had lost.

I now had knowledge. I didn't feel as lost when having to deal with a crisis at school. I could now say to the school "That's not appropriate for my daughter's education." On occasion I found myself saying "I looked this up on the Office for Civil Rights (OCR) web-site and what's there doesn't coincide with what you're telling me. Why don't we look that up and see?" It's amazing how fast members of a school district come to attention with just the mention of OCR. It's not so amazing that, the few times I've used that statement, the school personnel have never bothered to look it up, but just agrees with my request.

I have to stop and say, though, I also had to learn that sometimes what I thought my child needed, didn't always coincide with regulations either. On those occasions I learned to compromise. I learned to pick my battles with the school district. Sometimes I had to follow the old saying "Don't sweat the small stuff."

It would have been so easy to just stay angry and blame the entire school for everything. In time, I learned, they have a job to do and most of the time they do it to the best of their ability. There really wasn't a single evil person that I grew to hate in that school, just instances that were the result of poor decision making within the district. I thought my daughter should be in the forefront of everyone's thoughts because of our struggles. In reality I'm sure almost everyone in the school was probably dealing with their own set of problems, or budget crises, or wondering if their job was safe in these new shifting times. Every school is made up of human beings, just like us, with their own lives.

Saying that, I strongly feel that, because they get paid to do the job they're doing, they should do it to the best of their ability. When they don't, it's the families with knowledge who can bring an issue back into focus to be dealt with appropriately.

For anyone reading this book, I highly recommend taking any workshop you can and attending support groups. If you have a computer, look for the answers there. Google or Twitter, but don't give up. Don't stop searching for answers. Get angry if you have to, but don't sit back and just accept. Even the most well meaning organizations make mistakes once in a while. It's our job to see that the mistakes don't become habit. Hold these organizations accountable. You'll find that you are a much stronger person than you think is possible. Don't let anyone tell you they can't help your child. Look up information, be informed and be prepared. If we as parents hold a school district accountable each time regulations aren't followed, we can make a change.

By the end of Libby's Sophomore year, I went from being the Mom that complained and got nothing accomplished for their child at school, to the Mom who when I walked through the school doors, once overheard a secretary in the office murmur to the other secretary. "Uh oh, the fecal matter's going to hit the rotating blade some where today."

I didn't look any different than I looked a year ago. I still smiled at everyone. I'm a firm believer that you get more flies with honey than with vinegar. The difference was I now had knowledge. I had learned my way around the scholastic red tape. I no longer accepted what the principal or a teacher stated was fact. I looked questions up and had the answers ready, before even speaking with that teacher or principal. I now knew my daughters rights and what rights I had as a parent. The school knew that I knew. Knowledge is such a powerful tool.

During the summer, between Libby's sophomore year and her junior year, Sharon Johnson gave Libby her "BIRK" (Brain Injury Recovery Kit). It's a big box that's loaded with color coordinated information, specifically designed for someone with mild TBI. The BIRK teaches the patient how to color code and prioritize their daily routine. It took nothing for granted. I was amazed at how simple the technique really was and watched Libby easily picked up the strategies. In learning how to prioritize, the most important things, that need to be done immediately, are color coded bright orange. The BIRK taught Libby how to use physical techniques to take the place of her memory. There was a bright orange string that she was to keep with her during the day. If she had to stop doing something in the middle of a project, she was to lay the string on top of what she was doing, training her brain once again to look for bright orange. The string would draw her attention back to what she'd been doing earlier, making it easier to get through the day without as many unfinished projects. It contained tapes that we followed together as a team while we filled out the assignments in the work notebook together. It was something we worked on through the summer, preparing for her junior year.

Some of the assignments were so simple, they were almost silly. We followed the directions and did them anyway. One assignment asked the TBI survivor to make two inch bricks out of modeling clay and, on each brick, to write a word that described a difficulty or a feeling that was affected by TBI. I thought, for sure, Libby would not want to do this project because it involved thinking about what she was going through. She surprised me and actually ran out of bricks and we had to make more. Then to add her own personal flair, Libby painted each brick bright colors and outlined each word in gold or black. I found a small metal bucket that was just big enough to hold all her bricks. It became her TBI bucket.

Occasionally I'd see her take the bricks out of her bucket. Turning them over in her hand one at a time, sometimes she would smile and say "Hmmm I remember when that bothered me." Once in a while she'd scowl and put that brick back into the bucket, without any comment. It was a way to face what had happened, see the improvements and remember what still needed to be worked on. I think it worked for Libby because she could put that bucket away and not think about it until she wanted to.

She too was learning how to take control of her own life again. Between the counseling she had gone through her sophomore year, the BIRK and now attending a monthly TBI support group, Libby was coming to terms with her injury. She would still get embarrassed easily in front of strangers, but she was learning to advocate for herself. Throughout learning all these new techniques, Libby continued to heal, a little bit at a time, but the healing never completely stopped, giving us hope.

One day at school near the end of her sophomore year Libby had a substitute teacher for Phys-Ed. Libby played until she felt the pressure in her head building and then went and sat down on the sidelines. Normally her gym teachers were well aware of Libby's limits and never questioned her. This time, the substitute insisted she return to class and participate. Libby started to explain that she wasn't required to participate, but instead of listening the teacher commented, "What's the matter, do you have a boo-boo?"

"Yes," Libby said back just as sarcastically. "It's called a traumatic brain injury. Go read my 504 Plan, if you need to understand more."

We were learning to accept the reality of what TBI can do and we too were coming out on the other side. Libby was starting to talk about college again. She made it through 10th grade, once again passing everything. Once again excelling in her music courses and skimming by in some of her core classes, but still passing everything. I was determined her junior year was going to be successful. This skimming by just wouldn't do. Libby could, not only pass, but be successful, if we could just get the teachers to understand how important it was to follow her 504 Plan.

I decided to test Libby's stamina that summer. Earlier in the year Libby had watched a television show about treasure hunting. She'd seen the show that described how to hunt Herkimer diamonds in Upstate New York.

"Mom, can we go and do that this summer?" Libby asked me.

It looked like a lot of back breaking work and way beyond what Libby was capable of, but I vaguely told her it looked interesting. She continued to talk about going to hunt for Herkimer diamonds, as spring progressed. Finally I promised her that if she could pass everything and keep trying, I'd take her up to Herkimer County and we'd hunt for the crystals for a couple of days.

Unfortunately Dave couldn't take the time off work, so Libby and I asked our friend Rebecca to go with us. Rebecca had been so supportive to both Libby and I since we'd become friends, I didn't hesitate to ask her. Rebecca had never vacationed without Willy, but he gave his wholehearted consent.

In August of 2008 we took our first official vacation since Libby's accident. We planned on staying for five days and reserved a hotel with a pool, close to all the mines. We scrounged up every hammer, trowel, bucket, gloves and work tools we thought we might need in the mines and headed out. The mines aren't like coal mines, deep in the ground where it was dark, cold and damp. These were on top of the earth. The mine owners would dig trenches, or bring in piles of rocks and dirt to the site, dumping the piles in rows. Some areas in the mine consisted of rock walls that required a pick and sledge hammer.

The weather was perfect. We spent our first day in the mines digging, pounding and shaking buckets of dirt through sieves looking for those elusive crystals. Libby held up pretty well, but decided right away that hammering and digging were just too physical and bothered her neck and back, so she sifted dirt. That evening, we peeled off filthy clothes, showered, too tired to eat much and headed for the pool. Libby was exhausted, but once she hit that cool, refreshing water, her spirits picked back up.

We did a little searching and finally found a mine that fit our needs. Rebecca and I dug, pounded and crawled over sharp rock piles, hour after hour, thoroughly enjoying the hard work, while Libby sifted and wandered often picking up diamonds that were just lying on the surface. It had rained early that morning, so the surface crystals sparkled, making picking easy. When she tired, she'd go to the car that was parked within sight and under shade trees, roll down all the windows and take a nap, often sleeping for several hours each afternoon. We'd quit around 4:00 p.m. and find a restaurant that didn't mind filthy, dirt covered women, eat a quick meal, then head back to the hotel pool and revive ourselves. We had so much fun we stayed two extra days. We came home with the blazer full of virgin rock, just knowing that the "big one" was hidden somewhere deep in one of our chosen rocks.

We came home with a shoe box full of treasures, great farmer tans, hand-made necklaces holding our favorite diamonds and the knowledge that we can still have fun. Taking a break from reality is sometimes just necessary. Knowing that, as we pounded, dug, crawled, sifted, and rinsed anything that sparkled, TBI took a back seat. We became two grubby women and a filthy teenage girl mixing it up with all the other crazy people who pounded, dug, crawled, sifted and rinsed along with us.

When we came home, I felt the need to contact Dr. Rogers again. It had been a year since he'd seen Libby and I was curious as to what he felt her rate of recovery was. I also constantly found myself questioning if what I was doing for Libby, was the right thing. Did I push too hard? Did I not push hard enough? Did I get so wrapped up in this injury; I'd forget that she was healing? Every once in a while I'd have to stop what I was doing and just double check with someone in authority. Dr. Rogers was that person. We made our appointment for the week before she was to start her junior year.

Dr. Rogers was curious about Libby's progress, too. He sat and listened as I talked about some of the difficulties she still experienced, along with the fact that Libby didn't seem to know when to stop and rest. She would get so wrapped up in her daily routine, she would still "crash" and be bedridden at times. Libby took offense to that and began to argue with me.

"So, what do I drop, Mom? Do I drop music? No, not if I want to go to college for music. Do I drop homework? No, not if I want to pass. Do I drop violin lessons? No, what do you suggest I drop?"

I looked at Dr. Rogers for help and saw him smiling. He said, "Libby, it sounds to me like you have so many balls in the air that you're juggling them. So, what happens when you drop one of those balls? Or what happens when those balls come crashing down around your feet?"

"Well, Dr. Rogers," Libby said, leaning forward with determination in her voice. "You just pick those balls back up and start juggling again."

It was the first time I heard Dr. Rogers laugh out loud.

"I have to tell you something Libby," he said smiling. "For a long time I watched you huddle on the couch, or sleep against your Mom while we had our sessions and I never got to know the real Elizabeth Parker. Today, for the first time, I see you." He sat back in his chair, scribbling with his pen for a moment and then looked up.

"Often times when a person sustains an injury like you have, they go to a dark place. Sometimes it takes the person years to come out of that place. Sometimes they never do. I can honestly say that you have passed through that dark place and have come out on the other side."

"So I'm better?" Libby asked curiously.

"Well, you are definitely improved dramatically. Before, I never got to see who you were and now I do and that's a big step."

I noticed that Dr. Rogers hadn't actually answered Libby's question. She wanted a "Yes" or "No". I knew she wouldn't be satisfied with a partial answer.

"But am I better?" She asked again, watching Dr. Rogers intently.

Smiling, he paused and once again, chose his words carefully. "Better isn't a word I like to use," he said and immediately Libby began frowning. "What I like to say is, yes, you're back. You're back to having a personality, you're back to having a sense of humor and you're back among the living again. So, go out and live. Find out what you want to do and how you want to live your life."

It still wasn't the answer Libby was looking for, but I think she understood it was the best she was going to get.

We discussed re-testing Libby, but Dr. Rogers didn't feel it was the right time yet and that she would still have some healing. He wanted to wait another year and see. He said, in the meantime, to continue to be diligent about her homework and the teachers. It was a small assurance that I was on the right track and was doing the right thing.

CHAPTER 15

Glitches

Libby started her junior year, once again full of determination to prove to everyone that she was getting better, and she was. Her friends that had slowly stopped calling her in 9th grade started calling again. There were even kids in school who had forgotten about Libby's accident. For the most part Libby went through her days at school just like any other student. She became irritated with me if I asked her if she was remembering to write in her agenda. She only used her color coding when it wasn't obvious to anyone else in her class. She refused to carry around her bright orange agenda, and instead placed an orange patch on the cover of a smaller one, enough to draw her eye to her book and remind her to write, but not enough to have anyone ask why that bright patch was there. She was becoming independent.

Through all of her strategies, she was still and foremost a teenager. Her biggest concern, sometimes, wasn't how to learn, but how not to look out of the ordinary from all the other students. Anything that drew attention to her, that wasn't positive and she was horrified. She was maturing. Even TBI couldn't stop the fact that she was growing up. It wasn't easy for her to learn strategies that made her stand out from the crowd.

I continued to encourage Libby not to throw away what techniques she learned. Dave and I thought about what we could do to keep Libby on track. We were out driving on a sunny September afternoon. Libby was home, sleeping, still trying to adjust to the school routine, when we saw a sign at the end of a driveway, "MAINE COON CATS".

"I wonder what they are?" I questioned Dave, as we read the sign together.

"Let's find out," he replied, and pulled into the long driveway. Luckily the owner was home and happily showed us her cattery which contained several batches of kittens of this breed. Then a tom cat came strolling out and I fell in love. He weighed twenty eight pounds. The woman explained about the breed and their abnormal size. I told her how much our daughter loved cats.

"We've been promising her a long haired black female for a while, but we can't find one," I said. Most of the cats we'd seen, so far had been tigers, all of different colors.

"Hmmmm, well, I happen to have one in our newest batch of kittens." the woman responded. "But they're so new, their eyes only opened yesterday and I haven't shown them to anyone yet."

She disappeared and soon came back with a basket containing five tiny kittens, not allowing us to touch them because they were still so new. She held the tiny black kitten up and showed us. Dave and I looked at each other and knew. This was going to be Libby's kitten. It would serve as a reward to her from us.

I have to admit, it was a real hard thing to actually pay good money for a cat, even though she came with papers, when we had a barn full of kittens, at any given time. This was special, though, and "Lyla Jane" came to our home as soon as she was old enough. I just hoped Lyla, made up, even a little, for what Libby still struggled with.

Libby was sixteen and wanted to be treated her age. She was extremely upset with us when she had her sixteenth birthday and immediately wanted Dave and me to take her to the motor vehicle department to get her permit. We refused. I was horrified to think of Libby behind the wheel of a car. There were just too many glitches in her memory and focus, yet, for me to feel comfortable with her having that responsibility.

We had a riding mower and one of Libby's chores was to mow our extensive lawn. It took her three hours just to complete the general mowing. I watched as she mowed and noticed that sometimes just out of the blue Libby would forget how to turn the mower on, or where the brake was. Twice that summer she'd crashed into our house. Generally, she did fine, but, every once in a while, she would just forget to put the mower deck down and drive around and around. Little things that just sent warning signals to Dave and me, that she was not ready to drive a car yet.

We had an ATV and Libby was allowed to drive that, too, but only in our open field. Our chocolate Lab, "Goober" loved to run with the four-wheeler. Libby would take him daily, out to the field, for a run and to do his business. It saved cleaning the yard from dog land mines and it was an outlet for our over-energized, not so bright, hundred pound canine. Libby loved taking Goober out for his runs, but, in typical teenage fashion, hated wearing a helmet. Often, I'd find her sneaking back into the house, after hearing the ATV, without a helmet. Whenever I'd catch her, I would always scold her, but to no avail. I would hear comment sarcastically, "Oh what's it going to do, give me a brain injury? Thanks, Mom, got one of those already." Or "Geesh, I was only gone five minutes and went round and round the same track. Nothing's in the way that's going to hurt me. Stop treating me like I'm handicapped." Or her favorite, "Sorry, I forgot!" with all the drama and sarcasm she could muster in those three little words.

Yep, Libby was a teenager. Some days she was just a typical teenager getting through her entire day without having to think too much about her TBI. Those days came more and more often, until Dave and I, too, would almost forget. But the minute I did that, something would reach out and smash that façade all to pieces.

She was taking Forensics in her junior year. It was a substitute class that was offered for those students who weren't majoring in science and since Libby wanted to avoid Mrs. Floorz classes at all costs, she decided Forensics was what fit the bill for her. She knew and liked the teacher.

Ms. Gleason was the volleyball coach for the school and Libby loved volleyball. She hadn't been physically able to keep up with the strenuous training, so Ms. Gleason had kindly asked Libby if she could be their official score keeper. It kept Libby involved in the sport, without asking her to be as physical as the other girls on the team. It helped integrate Libby back into the mainstream school functions, helped out the volleyball team and, in a big way, made Libby feel part of things again. Libby did decide though, that she would pass on score keeping in her junior year.

I'd had several conversations with Ms. Gleason in the past regarding Libby's TBI and was comfortable with this teacher from the start. However, one afternoon, Libby came home from school, right before five week reports were due, announced she was failing forensics and that she hated the teacher. I asked her what the problem was.

"She's mean and keeps picking on me in front of everyone in class," Libby said dramatically.

"Libby, I thought you and Ms. Gleason got along great." I said, not quite falling for all the drama.

"Yea, we did until I told her this year that I wasn't helping out with volleyball." Libby had decided to not keep score this year, mainly because Dr. Alfred, her private violin coach, told Libby that playing volleyball can damage a violinist's hands permanently. Libby took that to heart and told Ms. Gleason, before volleyball season, that she was not going to help. Yes I know, she wasn't playing, but tell that to a sixteen-year-old that already knows everything and wants to hear nothing Mom or Dad has to say anymore.

As it turned out, the drama was very real. Ms. Gleason had refused to accept any late work from Libby since the day they'd had the volleyball conversation. I e-mailed her asking if there was a problem I wasn't aware of and received a very short, but to the point response stating that it wasn't fair to the other students. Her policy was NOT to accept any late work so therefore she wasn't going to accept Libby's.

It didn't matter that Libby's 504 Plan clearly stated that late work was to be accepted. Ms. Gleason was refusing. I then e-mailed her and said I'd be discussing this with Mr. King. I got a response from the teacher stating that possibly she'd over reacted and that she would indeed accept the late work.

Two weeks later, I got the five weeks report to find Libby had a 55 in Forensics. When I questioned Libby she said. "Mom, I already told you. Ms. Gleason won't take my late work and I keep getting zeros. I'm just not going to pass because I keep forgetting to hand my work in." Libby shrugged in resignation.

This time, when I wrote the teacher, I received a very cold response, absolutely refusing to accept Libby's work. I asked for a list of the missing homework, because I wanted to see if Libby was actually doing the work or using this as an excuse not to finish her assignments. I found that six assignments had received zeros for being late.

When Libby searched her room and book bag, she found all six assignments. Four of them were complete and two were finished to the rough draft.

When I asked Libby why, she said. "Because, when I asked her if I could turn it in tomorrow, Mrs. Gleason said, 'No Way'. So, I figured there wasn't any sense in finishing something she wouldn't take anyway."

I immediately contacted the CSE office and spoke with the chairperson telling her that they had a teacher that wasn't in compliance with Libby's 504 Plan and wanted it resolved. When I received the call back from the CSE office, I was told that Ms. Gleason would now accept the homework. So Libby trucked off to school, the next morning, ready to turn in all six assignments, only to have her come back home ready for a meltdown, because Ms. Gleason had scolded her in front of the class She insinuated that Libby was "special", because she got privileges the other students couldn't have. Libby still had the assignments in the book bag. Ms. Gleason was going to make an example of Libby to the rest of the class. When I checked my e-mail I had a letter from Ms. Gleason telling me that I'd misunderstood the CSE office and she absolutely would NOT take Libby's late work.

Within twenty four hours I'd arranged a general meeting that consisted of Dave, Libby, me, the CSE chair, Mr. King and Ms. Gleason. I was prepared to do battle once again. This time as the CSE chair and Mr. King tried to keep the meeting running smoothly, Dave and I spoke directly to Ms. Gleason. We informed her that she was not in compliance with Libby's 504 Plan and it didn't really matter what *her* class policies were, they took a backseat to any 504 Plan. It took almost an hour of bantering, back and forth, with Ms. Gleason's eyes literally sparkling with anger and stubbornness.

Finally I turned to Mr. King. "I think this meeting is getting us nowhere. Ms. Gleason obviously doesn't understand that what she's doing, can get this school in trouble. I'm going to leave that to you to explain the situation to her. In the meantime, I'm going to contact the Office for Civil Rights and file a complaint against this teacher and the school. You and I both know she can't just sit there and say, too bad so sad to us. You're obviously doing nothing to correct the situation, so I will."

I rose from my seat and gathered my notebook, as Dave and Libby stood.

"What do you mean by that?" asked Ms. Gleason, still angry, but I could see her eyes were darting between me and Mr. King.

"I mean that what you're doing is against the law, and I'm not going to stand for it." I said, just as calmly as I could, despite the fact that my hands were trembling.

Finally, Sandy Reynolds, the CSE chair, cleared her throat. "Ms. Gleason, I think we can come to a compromise here and resolve this without going outside the school district, don't you?" Though her voice had been pleasant, it held a warning that was clear to everyone in the room.

"So what do you want me to do? Just accept the work?" Ms. Gleason spoke, her voice now trembling.

"Yes, that's what we're asking you to do. Of course we can't force you, but I'm sure you want to clear this matter up as much as the Parkers, Mr. King and I do." Again Sandy spoke clearly, with that smile pasted on her face.

"I think this matter is settled as far as Libby is concerned." Mr. King said, nodding his head at Sandy. "And I don't think there will be any need to involve anyone beyond this office. Right, Ms. Gleason?"

"So Libby can bring in her work tomorrow for a grade and in the future this will no longer be in question, right?" I asked, looking at Mr. King.

"Exactly," he said, and escorted Dave, Libby and me from the room.

I have no idea what was said to Ms. Gleason after we left, but the work was accepted, every single late assignment. Anytime we went to the school for a function after that and Ms. Gleason was present, as soon as she saw us, she would leave our area, avoiding any more conversations.

Libby's grades improved a little in her junior year. She still struggled with Algebra, in spite of having a very compassionate teacher, and continued to receive low grades, sometimes below passing.

Again, because of the low Forensics grade we felt the repercussions. Libby received an Academic Ineligibility paper telling her because she'd failed two classes, she wasn't eligible to participate in NYSSMA. Solo Fest or NYSSMA is when music students perform a solo in front of a judge and receive grades. The higher the student's grade, the bigger the possibility of being asked to participate in All County, Area All State and All State performances. Libby had been participating in all since 6th grade and now she couldn't go. I confronted the school, again reminding them that it wasn't Libby's fault that she'd received failing grades in Forensics, but because of her Math grade, Mr. King refused to budge and wouldn't let her go.

It wouldn't have done any good for me to fight, because NYSSMA would have been over before The Advocacy Center or anyone else in authority, could have contacted our school to change the matter. I explained to Libby that she had to work harder to keep her grades up in all her classes to avoid this happening again. Sometimes you win and sometimes you lose. That's just life, though it burned me to think that she would have gone if it hadn't been for the Forensics crisis. I also learned to be specific when asking for accommodations. Libby had actually received a fifty on each of those six assignments. I didn't ask for a passing grade.

CHAPTER 16

Nurse Ratchet's Demise

In March, I could see that Libby was once again fading. Her fatigue was starting to take control of her again. Her migraines were increasing too. She was sleeping more, arguing more and smiling less. She'd missed a week of school in February because she'd come down with pneumonia. Since then, it seemed as if Libby was fighting an uphill battle to catch up. The stress was taking its toll on her.

She was going to the nurse more for her meds and missing more classes because of fatigue and migraines. Her grades had dropped an average of ten points since her bout with pneumonia, which put her back in that borderline pass/fail situation I dreaded so much.

On Monday, the first week of March, I received a call from Libby telling me she was out of Zomig, the prescription that she kept at school for migraine headaches. Zomig worked well for Libby, because it didn't cause sleepiness, like her other prescription Midrin. Midrin actually worked better to get rid of the headache, but, if Libby took it, it was almost impossible for her to stay awake and focused. So Zomig was the choice while at school, even though the school was required to carry both.

Since it was past lunch time, I told Libby to just go ahead and take her Midrin. If she couldn't stay awake just to go to the nurse and take a nap, then ride the bus home.

"Mom, won't you just come get me?" I don't like sleeping here," Libby said stubbornly.

In February and March, we had contractors at the house. I was getting a new kitchen and family room. Libby's bedroom and the spare room were also getting an overhaul. It was exhausting, stressful, and exciting, because I'd waited seventeen years for that new kitchen. On that particular day, the contractors were putting in my new cabinets.

"Honey, I can't. The guys need me here to show them which cupboard belongs where. I can't leave. You'll just have to deal with it at school, this time, and ride the bus home."

"Please…, can't you come get me?" Libby pleaded.

"No!" I was trying not to be angry at Libby, but there was just so much going on. As I spoke to her on the phone, the men were holding a cabinet, looking at me, waiting for me to end my conversation. "Just do what I ask and no more teasing!"

"But, what if I fall asleep and miss the bus?" Libby tried one more time.

"Elizabeth! Tell the nurse to make sure to wake you up. You won't miss the bus. Now stop teasing. I can't leave or the guys have to quit for the day. I want my cabinets in, so I can have my kitchen back."

"But…"

"No buts, Libby just do what I'm asking. Do you want me to talk to the nurse?" I watched the men finally set the cabinet down in the middle of the floor.

"No…"

"Good," I said hurriedly. I've got to go now; you can do this without me today. OK?"

"Ooo-kaay," Libby said, and hung up the phone without saying good-bye.

It was one thirty in the afternoon and Libby only had a little over an hour of school left. It wouldn't hurt to have her be responsible, once in a while, and know that Mom can't always be there at her beck and call. After all, she was seventeen now. Even though all that made sense, I felt just a pang of guilt as I turned back to the men and we continued working in my soon-to-be, brand new kitchen.

At three thirty, which was Libby's normal time for the bus to arrive, the phone rang. I ran to answer it as my husband walked in the door with another box of cabinets.

"Hello." I said, as I watched Dave set down the box and begin to open it.

"Mom, its dark in here and nobody's here." Libby sobbed into the phone.

"Libby, where are you?" I asked, as panic started consuming me.

"I'm at school, in the nurse's office. I'm all alone in here and the lights are all off," Libby said, still crying. "Mom, come get me."

"Honey, can you get out?" I asked?

"Wait let me see…" I heard her put the phone down and I waited. "Yep the door opens, but if I go out I can't get back in. It locks from the other side…What do you want me to do?"

"Honey, see if anyone is outside the nurses' office." I suggested, and waited as she went to the door again.

"No, nobody's around. The hall is dark too, but I can get outside because I know the doors to the outside don't stop us from getting out, only in."

"OK, Libby, make sure you have your book bag and everything you need out of the nurses office. Go stand just inside the door, where you can see us when we pull up." Anger was building inside me, knowing that exactly what Libby had feared, had come to fruition. The nurse had obviously forgotten Libby was asleep, on the cot, and locked the office before going home for the day.

"Ok, Mom, are you mad at me? I didn't miss the bus on purpose. I promise I asked the nurse to wake me up. She must have forgotten."

"I know, honey, I'm not mad at you, but wait till I talk to the nurse tomorrow. She's going to get a piece of my mind this time." Dave and the men stood there, watching me, waiting for an explanation. I quickly whispered to Dave that the nurse had left Libby alone in the office, shut off the lights and gone home.

"I'll go," Dave said, anger written all over his face. "Wait till I get my hands on that woman." he said, throwing on his coat and slamming the door.

The men looked at me with eyes wide, not saying a word.

"Honey, don't worry about a thing, Daddy's on his way now."

"Is he mad?" Libby asked. I'm sure she could hear Dave from her end of the phone.

"Yep, he really is, but not at you, at the nurse for being so forgetful." I said, trying to sooth her. Libby was afraid of the dark, and of being alone. Normally when she took Midrin, sometimes she slept four to six hours. I was really glad she'd woken after only two. What if she'd slept until 5:00 p.m. or 6:00 p.m., which she easily could have? It would have been completely dark out and she wouldn't have known where she was. At least there was still daylight outside so the inside of the nurse's office may have been dark and gloomy, but Libby could at least see to get around.

I hung up the phone promising Libby that her father would be there as soon as he could. I told her not to worry, even though I was livid.

Five minutes later the phone rang again and this time it was the nurse, Karen Barnes.

"Oh my GOD, Naomi, I'm so sorry," she said, with real fear in her voice. "I can't believe I did that. I just want you to know that, as soon as I remembered, I came right back. I promise I was only gone for three minutes tops."

"Don't give me that!" I said anger building even more at the lie. "Libby has to get on her bus at 2:50. She called me at 3:30. That's 40 minutes minimum that you forgot that you were responsible for my daughter's welfare. You do know that Midrin is a controlled substance, and you left her alone? How could you!"

"I know, I know. I deserve anything you want to say to me. I swear this has never happened before and I promise it will never happen again." Karen's voice trembled. "What do you want me to do? Do you want me to wait until you get here?"

It was then I remembered Dave's fury as he slammed out the door. I was tempted to say yes just to give Dave someone to unload on when he got to the school, but common sense took over.

"Look Karen, Dave's on his way and will be there in about ten minutes. If you know what's good for you, you'll get out of there before he pulls up." I warned her.

"Really, Naomi, if you want me to stay, I will. I deserve it," she said.

"Hmmmm, no, I think you better leave while you can. You don't know my husband. If you stick around, I may end up bailing him out of jail and I think we've had enough drama for one day." Though I was seriously tempted to just let Dave do what Dave does best, the father lion protecting his pride, I told her to go.

When Libby and Dave arrived home, Libby had calmed down and Dave seemed fine too. Libby came up to me and hugged me and said. "I told Mrs. Barnes the same thing about Dad."

I kissed her on the forehead, as I continued to squeeze her tight.

"You did, huh?"

"Yep, she told me she'd stay with me until Dad got there, but after she got done talking to you, she looked really scared. I told her she better run while she can, because when Dad gets mad she wouldn't want to be around for that." Libby giggled, squeezed me and smiled at Dave. All was right in her world again.

The next morning, I arrived at the school early, taking more Zomig into the nurse. As soon as I walked in the door, Karen jumped up from her seat behind her desk and came towards me with her arms open. I had no intention of comforting this woman and before she could wrap me in her arms, which I'm sure was her intention; I put my hands up in front of me to ward her off. She stopped instantly and began crying.

A young man was standing in front of her desk, signing in, and looked at both the nurse and I in total confusion.

"I'm so sorry, Mrs. Parker; you can't imagine how sorry I am," she said sobbing.

I folded my arms across my chest and just stared at her coldly.

"Really, I am. I promise I will take full responsibility for this. I'll go to the Superintendent and Mr. King and tell them both; you won't have to do a thing. I'm just so sorry!" She continued to cry.

She must have finally noticed the young man standing, frozen, in front of her desk, because she looked at him then at me. "Hold on a sec," she said to me, and just as quickly as she had turned on her tears, they disappeared as she turned to the student and coldly said. "GET OUT".

He ran past us, as fast as he could, and she locked the door behind him. Then, there they were again, the tears streaming down her face. I was disgusted at what I was witnessing.

"Here's all the Zomig I have in the house. I don't want Libby to run out again." I said, dumping the container of pills out on her desk. "You should count them, so the next time she gets down to one or two, maybe you can give me a call and let me know she's getting low, rather than running out again," I said with sarcasm.

As Karen counted out the pills and marked them in her med book, she continued to cry and said, "Really, whatever you say to me I deserve. You can yell at me all you want."

"Why? So you can feel better?" I asked derisively. "I don't think so. It's not my job to make you feel better; it's yours to make Libby feel better. This is supposed to be her safe place and now she won't feel safe here anymore. I'm only going to say this. You better fix this with her, because if I know my daughter, she'll stop coming for her meds and she can't do that."

"I promise I'll fix it. I'll get her a card or something. I promise she can feel safe here. This will never happen again, I swear, and I promise I'll take this matter to the supervisors myself. I will fix this."

"You better" was all I said as I walked out the door.

I decided not to talk about the situation in front of Libby because she would take Dave's and my anger and expand on that with the nurse. Libby still needed to come here. The school had insisted that, if her fatigue got too bad or she had a headache, Libby had to come to the nurse whether she liked it or not. I felt I'd made my point with Karen and hoped she really would patch things up with Libby.

On Friday morning, I got a call from Libby telling me she'd forgotten some homework at the house asking me to bring it down to school. When I hesitated, wondering for the hundredth time if covering for her memory impairments was actually helping Libby or hurting her, she then said that I needed to bring $12.00 down too.

When I asked her what the money was for, she stated it was for the admission for NYSSMA that she hadn't been able to attend. Then Libby explained that, if a student doesn't go, the parents have to be responsible for the money that the school submits on that student's behalf. In other words, the school wanted reimbursement for something that they'd refused to let Libby attend. I laughed and told Libby to have her music teacher call me.

Five minutes later the music teacher called and as politely as I could, or maybe not so politely, I informed her that if she wanted a refund, then she needed to get it from Mr. King, since he was the one that didn't let Libby go. I suggested that, since it was his decision, she should just ask him for the money because she wasn't getting it from us. When the teacher said she'd bring that matter up to Mr. King, I said "By all means, please do," and we hung up.

It took me about fifteen minutes to calm down and begin to think reasonably. Music was what kept Libby in school. Music was what had gotten her through the worst parts of recovery. Was $12.00 really worth taking a chance that now this teacher too would treat Libby as the enemy? I thought about it and decided that it just wasn't worth it, so I placed the money in an envelope, found Libby's homework and headed for school.

As soon as I walked through the office door, Mr. King came out of his office. He greeted me with a huge artificial smile pasted on his face. In an overly jolly voice, he asked, "And how are we today Mrs. Parker?"

In just as sugary a voice as I could, I answered. "I'm not doing well at all today Mr. King, how about yourself?" I smiled just as broadly at him.

"Why, it sounds like we need to have a talk, don't you think?" he said.

By this time every eye in the office was bouncing back and forth between the principal and me, like a tennis match. Everyone knew something was up.

"Why, yes, I agree," I said, still smiling like it was the most wonderful day in the world. He motioned me into his office and closed the door behind me.

Surprisingly, he continued to smile as he sat down in his chair while I sat in the one placed in front of his desk.

"So, tell me what's going on. I've already heard Mrs. Hayes's side and your suggestion." he said, continuing to smile, though his voice had quieted in seriousness.

I explained that I had been upset at the thought, that after the school refused to let Libby attend Solo fest, they'd have the audacity to ask for their money back. I reminded him that if it hadn't been for Forensics, Libby would never have been placed on Academic Ineligibility because, according to the school's policy, a student had to be failing two subjects, and he agreed.

"So, why would you even think that I'd be willing to refund the school?" I asked now a little confused, because Mr. King still continued to smile.

"Well, let me make something clear." he said quietly, going back to his principal voice. "I had no idea that our school even had this refund policy. Apparently this is something that the music department has designed and I was never made aware of. Also, I want you to know that I'm not fond of this policy at all."

Ahh, so now this was beginning to make sense. I discussed the fact that I was willing to pay the money just because I wanted to keep the peace between the music department and Libby. I didn't want her paying for our differences.

Mr. King assured me that he wouldn't let that happen. He then suggested that we go to the new superintendent, who had been hired when Mrs. Crabner suddenly resigned. He felt that Mr. Johnson needed to be aware of this policy and that, more than likely, a policy change was in order.

It was then that I decided to ask Mr. King about the nurse's incident that had happened on Monday. "Mr. King, before we call him, I have something else I'd like to ask you?"

"Sure, go ahead," he said, placing his phone back in its receiver.

"Well, I was wondering if you'd had any discussion with the nurse this week?" I asked tentatively.

"You mean about Libby? No. I've talked with her several times this week, but nothing about Libby, why? Has something happened?"

"She promised me she'd come to you." I said, genuinely surprised that Mr. King knew nothing. Then anger started building again, as I realized that Karen had said all she'd said to me, just to keep me from talking to administration. She never had any intentions of telling anyone.

As I told him what happened, I watched as he slowly leaned back in his chair, placed his hands on his head and slowly rubbed them back and forth through his hair, while his face grew redder and redder. As I continued my story, he began shaking his head and sighed deeply.

"Mrs. Parker, I am really sorry. But Karen did NOT come to me. This is a very serious situation and needs to be dealt with. Now I really think we need to see Mr. Johnson. He needs to be informed of this." He picked up the phone, spoke with the receptionist a minute, replaced the receiver and opened his office door for me.

As we walked out into the office, Karen walked in, smiled and said "Hi," as if nothing had ever happened. I noticed the change of expression as her gaze moved to Mr. King. She went white as we walked by her without another word.

When we got to Mr. Johnson's office we were introduced. I wondered what he thought about us and wondered how much he'd been informed about our lawsuit and all the problems we'd had the past several years with the school. He gave me a genuine smile and shook my hand firmly, though. I immediately liked him.

As I began to recount my story, once again, though, his smile disappeared and he became deadly serious.

"Mrs. Parker, I'm sorry this happened to Libby, but I have to say, you didn't do us any favors by waiting to tell us this."

"I know, Mr. Johnson, but Karen promised me she would tell you herself and I wanted to give her that opportunity." He nodded in understanding, and assured me without hesitation, that this matter would be dealt with. We then talked about the money the music department wanted refunded to them. He assured me that he would take care of that matter and I would not be required to pay anyone.

The following week, Libby and I were interviewed by an investigator. We both recounted the incident in the nurse's office to her. The investigator asked if we'd ever had any other instances with this particular nurse. Libby immediately brought up the fact that the nurse had told her she was Bi-polar and that the nurse and her mom had gotten into an argument over it. I simply said. "It was not her place to diagnose my daughter. Libby has a doctor for that." I quickly explained that Libby had mild TBI and what had happened with the nurse. The interview lasted about an hour. The investigator was very polite and the following day Nurse Ratchet no longer was employed at the school. Again the gag order was put out to all teachers and employees, but for the rest of the year, a substitute nurse filled in.

CHAPTER 17

The Breaking Point

There comes a time, in the life of a caregiver, when it becomes too much. That time came for me when Libby was finishing her junior year. Even though the year went somewhat smoother, we still had some rough patches that needed attention. I think, though, when the nurse forgot Libby and we had to speak with the investigator that was the proverbial straw that broke the camels back for me. From that moment on, I found my temper was short and my patience was even shorter.

Sharon Johnson again reminded me that the Brain Injury Assoc. was having their annual conference in Albany. This year I registered both Libby and I. I hoped the conference would give me the serious boost of energy I needed to keep going. My emotions were high and so were Libby's. I hoped the conference would give us that little time away and a chance to refresh and renew our determination to keep going.

I found that Lee Woodruff was the key speaker. I couldn't wait to hear her speak. I had read her book "In an Instant" that was about her husband Bob's tragic accident and his recovery.

I was still thinking about writing my own book. I hoped to get a few pointers if not from her, at least from BIANYS. I also wanted Libby to meet some of the people I'd met the year before. I hoped the school wouldn't give us too much trouble about Libby missing classes, but I felt this was important and just might be what Libby needed to show her that TBI didn't have to be a death sentence. She could recover and lead a normal life. I contacted the school and waited for their answer.

Libby and I started arguing more about little things. I know if I'd had better control of my emotions, I could have avoided most of the arguments. She pressured Dave and me more and more to get her permit. We finally gave in, as long as she understood that there were rules. No radio, no cell phone on, only one person in the car with her and absolutely no friends while she drove, until both Dave and I felt she was ready. I discussed it with Dr. Rogers and he agreed that it was time for Libby to drive, providing she agreed to the rules. Naturally she agreed to anything as long as it meant she could drive so off to the DMV we went and Libby came home with her permit. I have to admit I am not the ideal person to be a passenger in a car with a first time driver, but I let Libby drive home, once we were past the major intersections. We made it home intact, but my not so subtle comment to Dave was "You are teaching her, I did my part." In turn, I got an "Ohhhh OK" and a sheepish grin, as I stormed into the kitchen.

Don't get me wrong, Libby actually did pretty well her first time driving. She kept her speed down even in the 55 mph zone. I'm just not cut out to be the patient, calm person that sits in that passenger seat and puts her life on the line in those beginning stages of learning to drive. I now admit it to the world, I am a control freak and not sitting behind the wheel is giving up total control. I just can't bring myself to sit there and stay calm as Libby drives about a foot away from guard rails, or takes that curve fast enough to push you against your door. I white knuckle it every time, while Dave just rides along, looking out into the fields and just lets her learn. So I happily gave up that responsibility to my husband.

I hoped that letting Libby get her permit would slow down some of the arguing that was going on between us, but it didn't. I think we'd just reached that place where she was growing up and away from me and was trying to assert her independence, while at the same time still clinging to me when she needed the moral support. So, the arguing continued as I tried to decipher if this fight was just a typical teenager/parent fight or was it a fight because there was an issue with her TBI that she just couldn't absorb or control.

I think our worst fight came at Easter time. I was having my entire family over for Easter dinner. I had run to the grocery store several times for ingredients in the past forty eight hours. Our grocery is a half hour away so I'd grown accustom to making a list and shopping once or twice a week. I'd already shopped my quota. There is a special dessert I make, that everyone loves. Its mini sponge cakes, with the center filled with fresh raspberries, raspberry preserve. It's then frosted with a lemon curd, cream cheese frosting and garnished with fresh raspberries, blackberries and more preserves. It's not that hard to make, but all the ingredients have to be fresh.

When I got home from the store I showed Libby the berries and said to her. "You can't eat these because I have to use them for my cakes in the morning OK?"

She gave me half a glance and mumbled, "Oh, OK," and left the kitchen. while I unpacked groceries.

The next morning, I noticed the blackberry container on the counter, empty, and looked into the fridge. Sure enough, there were no blackberries.

"Libby, get out here now." I called sternly.

She meandered out into the kitchen, as I held out the empty container to her.

"What is this?" I asked

"Huh?" she said. "Looks like a berry container to me, why?"

"Libby, I specifically told you not to eat these yesterday. Now I have to run to town again to get more." I angrily stuffed the empty container into the trash as Libby looked at me defensively.

"No, you didn't, you said "don't eat the raspberries" so I didn't."

"No, I said, "Don't eat these." I showed both of them to you."

As we started our first argument of the day, I suddenly stopped, threw up my hands and decided it just wasn't worth fighting about. "Never mind, I'll go get more."

I grabbed my coat and stormed out the door.

Was she not paying attention? Didn't she see both berry baskets in my hands? Or did she just eat them because she wanted them, and in typical teenage fashion, do what she wanted, in spite of what I'd said.

I was still fuming one and a half hours later as I got home and prepared to make my cakes.

"Libby, come here." I called to her

She came out of her bedroom warily looking at me as I held a basket in each hand.

"See this?" I asked and then switched hands to the other basket in front of her "And see this? Do NOT touch these."

"Ooh Kay," Libby said, dramatically rolling her eyes at me.

"I mean it, Libby; I'm not going to the store again, got it?"

"Yea, I got it," she said, just as angrily back at me

I stormed around my kitchen, putting my groceries away, and started my cakes. Some of the berries I had to save for the next morning, so the topping would look fresh. I used what I needed for now and put the rest back in the fridge.

The next morning as I got up early to prepare the lamb and the rest of the foods, before family came, I saw an empty berry container, once again on the counter. I threw open the fridge and yep, all the raspberries were gone.

"Elizabeth Rose Parker, get your butt out here, now." I yelled as loud as I could.

What a wonderful start to Easter morning.

She came stumbling out of her room, wiping sleep from her eyes.

"Wha-at?" She asked, looking at me as if I'd lost my mind.

"Tell me, young lady, what this is?" I said shoving the berry basket at her.

Rolling her eyes, she calmly said, "You said "Don't eat the blackberries," so I didn't. Now what's wrong?"

"I showed you both, you know that. Libby I can't believe you ate them!"

"Mom, I only ate the ones you said I could. I didn't touch the blackberries." Libby said, her eyes filling with tears.

The anger left me as suddenly as it came on me. I was yelling at someone who didn't understand. Here she was, standing in front of me, with tears in her eyes, telling me she was only doing what I'd told her to do. Obviously my method of shoving things in her face didn't work. If I'd thought like a caregiver I'd have simply taped a note to each basket that said "DON'T EAT ME." We'd have never even have had this fight.

"Go back to bed Libby." I said resigned to the fact that once again we'd fought over something that was really nothing. Of course by then, Dave was in the kitchen wanting to know what all the commotion was about and was kindly offering to go get more berries. Did I really need raspberries? No, not really, the cakes would look just as nice with only blackberries on the top. I felt truly ashamed.

My shame became exhaustion and resignation as Libby spent the rest of the holiday steering clear of me. This was supposed to be a time of rejoicing. I'd ruined it for Libby and me.

Later in the week, I received a call from Frank Walker, our attorney, with not great news. He calmly told me that our case just didn't look that good anymore. He stated that he'd done everything he could to show the courts that Libby had a legitimate injury, but without that concrete piece of evidence, such as an X-ray or CAT scan, or MRI showing something, Libby's case just didn't look promising. The opposing side had filed a motion with the court to have everything dismissed, because there was no concrete evidence. We talked about expert witnesses, which we'd already spent thousands of dollars hiring and Frank simply said we stood about a fifty-fifty chance of getting our case thrown out of court even before it went to trial.

I was devastated. I was angry because anyone that knew us, knew the truth. Because New York State laws are written that to show a permanent injury you have to have that concrete evidence, we may lose before we even got to trial.

That afternoon when I got the mail, Libby's five week report arrived and I opened it. She was failing two subjects and one was Forensics. Apparently, Ms. Gleason hadn't put Libby's back homework in that she'd accepted and graded. When I checked with the school she actually had, but Libby had only been given a fifty for each homework assignment. Once again, Libby would be placed on Academic Ineligibility. It was April.

Her prom was in May and Libby had plans to go. If she was on Ineligibility, she couldn't go. She'd missed Soph Hop in 10th grade because of poor grades and had already missed NYSSMA and now prom? I just couldn't take it anymore.

I sat in our chair by the phone, dropping all the mail. I didn't even have the energy to pick it up. Tears poured down my cheeks as I sobbed gut wrenching sobs. I just couldn't do this anymore. I couldn't be the strong one, the one to always handle everything, the one to comfort Libby when she had a bad day, confront the school when there was a problem. Was this never going to end?

I loved my daughter, desperately. How could I feel like this? I loved my husband, but at that moment resented him for every time I picked up the flack. I dealt with schools, and was the one to talk with attorneys. I wanted to scream at the world, but I just didn't have the energy to even get out of my chair, so for two hours I cried and sobbed and made myself sick, because I just couldn't stop. Finally, I dragged myself up out of the chair, up the stairs and crawled into bed.

Libby found me there when she got home from school.

"Mom, what's wrong? Are you sick?" Libby asked standing in my bedroom doorway.

"I don't feel well. You'll have to take over and make supper tonight." I managed to get out, before tears started welling up again.

"What about orchestra? We have to leave in an hour," she asked.

"Not tonight Libby, I just can't. If Dad gets home from work in time, he can take you and if he doesn't, you'll just have to miss. Please shut the door, Honey, I just need quiet." I pulled the covers over my head, trying to shut out the world.

Dave came up to the bedroom when he got home and saw the shape I was in. Quietly he left, taking Libby to orchestra and out to dinner. Several times, after they got home, both Dave and Libby came to check on me. Once, Libby brought me fresh brewed, mint tea and lay down on the bed with me for a minute. I kissed her forehead and thanked her, but even that gesture brought tears again.

The following day, after spending most of the day in bed, I finally managed to pull myself together enough to tell Dave about the lawyers and Libby's grades. I'd stayed strong for so long, sure that everything would work out, as long as I held up my end of the bargain. That's what I thought, and to have everything just come crashing down in less than a week, was just too much.

I mentioned to Dave that maybe I needed some of Libby's "happy" pills, because I was running out of steam, fast. He left the room after a while and came back with the cordless phone.

"Someone wants to talk to you," he said.

"Dave, I don't want to talk to anyone, just handle it," I said, rolling over in bed, putting my back to him.

I found the phone, dropped on my pillow just in front of my face, as he quietly said, "Nope."

"Hello." I said, dully, into the phone.

"Well, Hello, Dah-h-ling," came the voice of my favorite cousin over the phone.

"Hi Babs," I said. "Did you need something?"

"Why, yes I do." Babs said, in an overly cheerful voice. "I need you to get your ass out of bed, get in the shower and dress up Doll, cause it's "martooni night."

I couldn't help it. I started smiling. Babette Jones and I had grown up together although for twenty years, we'd lived on different sides of the continent. When she moved back to the area a couple years before, we fell back into that old friendship, as if time had never passed. She was eccentric, bold, and knew how to get her way. I'd never learned how to say "no" to Babs. And she was right. She was just what I needed.

"I'll be there in an hour. Tell that husband of yours, he's DD tonight." Without another word the phone went dead. I heard a rustling behind me and saw Dave standing there, sheepishly looking at everything in the room but me.

"Bab's will be here in an hour. I guess you're going with us as designated driver." I said with a lightness I hadn't felt in two days. I got out of bed, found some decent clothes and headed for the shower, while Dave stood rooted to his spot in the bedroom grinning. His smile widened, even further, as I stared at him and casually threw out. "It's martooni night."

I won't go into the gory details of how "martooni night" got started but suffice it to say, it had become a signal to us, through the years, that it was time to have fun and stop worrying about the rest of the world.

Babette and I didn't see each other often, but when we did, we always had fun. Dave couldn't have picked a better person to call than Babs to pull me out of my depression. As I walked past him with my arms full of clothes, I kissed him and said. "Thanks, I needed her."

True to her word, Babs arrived. But, knowing Bab's as both Dave and I did, we didn't hurry. She was notoriously late for everything. She didn't let us down. She pulled in the drive, and rolled down her window, "woohoooing" us to "Let's get this party started."

For the first time, in a long time, Libby didn't even ask where we were going, but just said. "Have fun, and Dad, you drive!"

Babette did what she does best. She made me laugh, told me I looked like Hell, and proceeded to order us each two double vodka martini's, with extra olives, as soon as we sat down at the bar. She never once asked me what was wrong, or offered advice on how to fix it. She loudly proclaimed, "We aren't leaving here until clothes start coming off!" while Dave pretended not to know us. Suffice it to say that Babette was in no shape to drive home, so we had our first sleep over since we were kids.

By Monday, I felt like I could interact with the human race again. As soon as I knew that the school offices were open, I called Sandy Reynolds, the CSE chair, and laid it on the line for her. My daughter was NOT going to miss prom if I had to walk her in myself and stand there. If they wanted to fight over it, I'd be happy to, but prom is a right of passage for every teenage girl. They weren't going to take that away from Libby. Sandy and I talked about Libby's grades. I started to fall apart for the first time in front of someone at the school.

"Sandy, I just can't do this anymore; pretend that everything is working when it isn't. I can't explain to Libby why she can't go to her prom, when it's just because certain teachers won't follow her 504 Plan."

She agreed with me. When I insisted on an emergency meeting, she said it wouldn't be necessary. She could make what ever changes we needed. I had no idea she had the authority to do that. Before our conversation was over, Sandy had implemented several new amendments to Libby's 504 Plan. She no longer would be in jeopardy of loosing credit for classes, when her missed school days caused the phase I and II letters. From now on, anything TBI related would be removed from her attendance record and wouldn't count. That meant she could attend the TBI conference in June. She also lowered Libby's passing to a 55 which would eliminate the ineligibility and Libby could go to prom.

Suddenly, I had an entirely different woman talking to me. She was full of suggestions. Sandy offered changes in the 504 Plan that would actually make Libby successful and we wouldn't have to worry so much about her passing. She also said she'd have a very stern talk with all Libby's teachers and put a stop to any non-compliance.

I hung up the phone, feeling elated. In just a half hour, I'd made more progress with the school than I had in two years. Maybe it was because of the school nurse incident, maybe not, but I wasn't about to look a gift horse in the mouth. I sat by the phone for a while just savoring the success.

I think, reaching the breaking point for me was necessary. It taught me some very good lessons. First, don't let yourself get to that point when you don't have too. I've since learned, when I get feeling like I'm losing control, I take a couple hours or even a couple of days and just stop. I don't have to be on my toes every minute of the day. I can relax, read a book, have a glass of wine and guess what? The world doesn't fall apart if I do. Libby needs me, but she also needs to learn independence. If I decide to go to the lake for the night with one of my sisters, Dave can handle whatever happens at home and Libby can learn to handle things by herself, too. I learned that Libby may or may not pass every class. If she doesn't, then she will just have to make some choices about her life and maybe some changes. I can't always be the one to fix everything. She has to learn to be accountable.

Libby and I attended the Brain Injury Conference. For two days we went to workshops together, had nice dinners and met wonderful people. I finally got to meet the woman that opened my eyes to what TBI is. I can't believe it, but I was actually nervous, standing in line for Lee Woodruff's book signing for her new book "Perfectly Imperfect." As we reached the table and Lee opened the book to write in it for Libby and me, I found myself telling her about that day, sitting on my sofa, listening to her story and what a difference it had made in the way I handled Libby's TBI. Before we knew it, we were both crying. Of course Libby was embarrassed because Mom had made the famous lady cry.

When Libby finished her junior year, she passed every regents exam except Algebra B. Her grade was so horrible, she wouldn't be able to retake it and pass the course, unless she got in the 90's on the exam. That was never going to happen. So instead she signed up for another math class in her senior year. As long as she passed that one she would still get to graduate with her Regents' diploma. Nothing I did or tried could make Libby remember Algebra.

I learned to let go, a little. Funny, when I finally learned that, Libby and I stopped arguing so much. Being a TBI caregiver isn't easy. For so long you're required to micro manage everything, remember for the person who can't, remind them to take their meds, push them when they need pushing, know when to back off, when fatigue becomes too much. Then one day, you realize that simple fixes are sometimes all you need. Tape the note on the food, sit back a little from the intensity of everything, and enjoy life when you get the chance.

The lawyers would do what they do and there was nothing I could do to change that. For two and a half years I'd carefully kept records, journals, dr. appointments, gone to work shops, conferences, support groups and it might just not be enough. Libby just may end up with nothing. If she did, the school could just say "too bad so sad" and all her accommodations could be gone in a flash. If it happened there wasn't a thing I could do about it. I'd done my very best and so had Dave and Libby. I was learning the hard way that justice isn't always served.

CHAPTER 18

Settlement

The phone rang a few hours after Libby left for school in early June. It was Frank with more news. He felt that we just might stand a chance of winning the case if Libby would go for more testing. He said he'd been in touch with some TBI experts and they felt that a pet scan might show damage to Libby's brain even when the other tests hadn't. He also told me that they were scheduling a new round of neuropsych testing because the school's attorney had said her testing was out dated. Apparently, there's a set of tests if the person is younger than sixteen and another set when they are sixteen and older. The opposing side was complaining, because Libby had never had these newer tests. They also wanted to meet with Libby's neurologist and see what she had to say. Frank said that it was important for us to do all of this because it showed that we weren't afraid of any test the opposing side might put Libby through.

Just as Libby started her junior year there had been a flurry of activity between our attorneys. The schools attorney demanded that she see an independent doctor. We made the long drive to

Syracuse. The exam was such a sham; it disgusted Dave, Libby and me. The doctor never even read Libby's file, had no idea what questions to ask us and just kept saying "So tell me…" He'd wait for us to fill in the blanks. He made Libby lie on her back and then told her to sit up. When she placed her elbow behind her, to assist herself, the doctor jerked Libby's elbow out, causing her to fall back on to the table. He pulled her flip flops off her feet and literally threw them against the wall beside me. The entire exam lasted ten minutes. That was the most bizarre appointment I'd ever seen and I had to refrain myself from walking out of his office as he jerked Libby around and made a fool of himself. This doctor was going to be one of the expert witnesses in the schools case telling a jury that Libby was faking. Frank had a representative come to the doctor appointment and film everything. At first, this doctor was so rude; we thought he might actually refuse to allow the filming.

About a week later, our own insurance company requested an independent medical evaluation and sent Libby to a doctor in a neighboring town. This doctor thoroughly read Libby's file, covered all her impairments and when we left assured us that we had nothing to worry about. Libby would continue medical treatment and the insurance company would continue to pay. Since that time, every six months, Libby has had to go back for her IME (Independent Medical Evaluation) with this same doctor. Every time this doctor would again reassure us that Libby's treatment would continue.

The things we had to do to pacify lawyers, sometimes were ridiculous, but we did them. This time, after I got off the phone with Frank, I looked up on the internet what a PET scan was and saw that the patient had to inhale radioactive fumes before the scan was performed. It stated clearly that women of child bearing age should avoid this procedure unless necessary. I panicked and called Sharon Johnson. We talked about the different procedures and she reminded me of another scan that was very successful in detecting mild brain injuries. It was called a DTI (Diffusion Tensor Imagine) scan. It was harmless compared to the PET scan, so I called Frank and Cheryl. I asked them if they could find a place for her to go for the DTI scan instead of the PET scan.

We made a visit back to the neurologist and I discussed it with her. She said that she thought the PET scan would be useless in detecting anything. It just might end up being another feather in the opposing sides' cap. Then she gave me the bad news. No DTI scans were available any where near driving distance for us. She did agree that if Libby had any scar tissue that was residual from her injury the DTI scan would probably pick it up. Unfortunately nobody had one.

The following week, we went to see Dr. Rogers again to schedule Libby's neuropsych testing. He explained that it would start at 9:00 a.m. and they probably wouldn't finish until at least 5:00 p.m. We left there with the promise that Dr. Rogers would call us as soon as his schedule allowed for a full free day.

On Monday, the last week of school for Libby, Frank called me again.

"Naomi, I have some surprising news," he said. "Are you sitting down?"

"Yes, Frank, I'm sitting down, what's the news." I said, not quite sure where this was heading. We were scheduled to appear in court the following week, to find out if the judge would allow Libby's case to go to trial, so I really didn't have any idea what good news he may have.

"Well, I just got off the phone with the opposing side and you're not going to believe this, but they want to talk about a settlement."

"Why now?" I asked Frank.

"Well, I'm thinking, that just maybe, they aren't as sure about winning as we are. I think agreeing to all those tests rattled them. I think they're getting nervous. If the judge approves Libby's case and allows it to go forward, they don't want that either. So, before it goes in front of the judge, they want to settle, as long as it's within reason."

"And within reason means what?" I asked. Through our entire lawsuit, Frank had never allowed a figure to be discussed.

He'd always said it could be a small amount or a big one, but never said what big was or small was. I remember telling Frank, at the very beginning, that if Libby came out of this after years of battling, with only a thousand dollars, I didn't want to pursue anything. It wouldn't be worth it and he agreed that if he felt it was ever headed that way, he'd stop. That was the only conversation we'd ever had about money.

"Well at this point they've offered $25,000, but I already told them "No way". Your fees are almost that much, so it would barely cover expenses and Libby would only be left with a couple thousand dollars."

"Absolutely, no way." I reiterated. "I'll see this all the way through before I let that happen," I said.

"I know Naomi, I already told them they weren't even in the ball park."

"Then what are you thinking?" I asked.

"I think if we can get a settlement of $40,000, then that will give Libby about $23,000 after expenses."

Frank seemed as pleased as punch. I wasn't. I just didn't feel right.

"Frank, I don't like it." I said firmly. "All that Libby's been forced to go through and this is what she'll end up with? Really I thought it would be closer to $100,000."

"Naomi, you probably wouldn't get that for her even if you went to trial and won." Frank said.

Suddenly I pictured Libby, in her senior year, with no accommodations and being at the mercy of school administration. I knew if we lost, that could be a very real possibility.

"I don't know what to do." I said. "Frank, let me ask you. You have kids. If it was your daughter, would you settle for that amount?"

Without hesitation, he answered "Absolutely, Naomi. I would take what I could in financial benefits and remember that it's a win for you. If you take it, the school is finally admitting to liability and can't take a single thing away from her."

"I'll have to discuss this with Dave and Libby before I agree to anything, but I can tell you honestly. I don't like that figure. I'd be much happier if it was higher," I said.

"And so would I because the more Libby makes the more I make, but remember when you're talking it over tonight, that this is a win for you."

Dave and I talked it over with Libby that night and we all agreed. Maybe, just because that figure just didn't set well with us, if Frank and Cheryl could get the amount to $50,000, we'd agree to take the deal.

The next morning I called Frank with our decision. He was rather short with me on the phone, but said he'd see what he could do.

Friday morning Frank called back, his voice filled with excitement. Once He'd turned down the $25,000 and the $40,000 offer, the opposing side said, that amount was all they were authorized to offer. Frank thought, for sure, we'd be going to the hearing next week. Two hours later the school's attorney called back with an offer of even more than we had asked for. Frank accepted it.

The legal red tape is ridiculous. Papers went back and forth between the attorneys for weeks. Then Frank called us with more news. The judge wanted to speak to us before he signed off on the settlement. Apparently it was this judge's policy to speak with the family of any child under the age of eighteen, so that meant another wait.

In August, we finally got to see the judge. Frank came with a cart of boxes piled to the top telling us "This is Libby's file." He was prepared to show anything the judge might ask to see. Frank informed Dave, Libby and me that the judge would probably talk to me about making sure I understood that this was Libby's money and not ours. He explained that, often, there was a problem when parents felt they should be compensated for their trouble too, but in cases such as this, it was strictly a pain and suffering case that went entirely to the person with the injury. He also stated, several times to us, that if we showed any doubt at all about the amount that Libby would be receiving, the judge had the ability to withdraw the offer and still send the case to trial or throw it out.

We walked into the court room as prepared as we could be for whatever questions the judge might have for us. We sat waiting, for about a half an hour, before our case was called up. Libby and I walked to the table, placed in the courtroom for clients and attorneys. Frank stood at a podium a little in front of us. He talked for a few minutes, to the judge, about Libby's accident and her injuries, explaining why we'd decided to take the settlement, clearly stating that because of lack of concrete evidence, he'd advised us to settle. He told the judge that it was as important to us to make sure that Libby's accommodations, at school, were still intact. He explained that when all this was over, accommodations were just as important to us as any monetary offer.

The Judge asked Frank a few questions regarding expert witnesses, then leaned back in his chair, and thought for a moment.

Crooking his finger, the judge said, "Elizabeth, would you come up here and sit next to me in this chair?"

Without hesitation, Libby immediately went to the witness chair and sat down. As soon she was seated, the judge leaned forward and spoke quietly to her. I could hear what he was saying, but clearly he meant his conversation for my daughter alone.

"Ok, Elizabeth, I understand that you were in an accident and hurt your head right?" Libby nodded her head yes. "Well I just wanted to tell you that now that this is over, now that you finally have settled, you don't have to have symptoms anymore. Do you understand?"

I gasped as I heard the judge, in not so subtle language; tell my daughter he thought she was faking. I had to clasp my hands together, in front of my mouth, just to remind myself to not say a word.

Libby looked at the judge in confusion and shook her head no.

"Ok, let me explain this again. A couple years ago, I was in an accident and I hurt my head too, only I didn't sue anyone. I got better fast. So, I'm telling you, that now that this is over, you can be better. Do you understand me now?" Again, Libby shook her head no as I sat there wanting to say something to put an end to all this nonsense.

"Ok, I'll try again. Sometimes, when you get hurt and you sue someone, your brain tells your body to stay hurt and you are afraid to get better. So, now that this is over, you can be better. Do you understand?"

This time Libby shook her head yes and said. "I guess so."

"Good, that's all I have to say then." The judge said, and motioned for Libby to get down from her seat. He reached for his pen and signed her agreement. Within a minute we stood outside the doors to the court room my head swirling from what I'd just witnessed..

"Guys," Frank said, shaking his head. "If you weren't sure that settling was the right thing, be one hundred percent sure now. That man did not believe Libby and would have thrown her case out. We'd have never stood a chance with him."

The doors opened behind us and the clerk walked over to Frank handing him the signed papers. He turned and smiled at Libby and said "So you can be all better now right?"

"Oh wouldn't that be just WONDERFUL!" I said to the clerk. How stupid can people get, was what I was really wanted to say. I turned back to Frank and Dave and saw Frank with his fingers over his lips cautioning me.

"I'm sorry Frank, but this is the kind of ignorance we've been dealing with for almost three years now."

"I know, Naomi," he said, trying to comfort me. He was as shocked as I was. Luckily Dave, who'd sat in the back of the courtroom, hadn't been able to hear what the judge said to Libby, or I know there would have been words.

"I will tell you this much. What he said was so inappropriate. He was interjecting personal opinion into a court case and he can't do that. I know this doesn't help Libby, but if I ever get another case like this, I will never let it be heard in front of this judge, ever. I'll file to have him recuse himself, because of what I heard him say today."

"What about that next person?" I asked Frank. "That sort of ignorance can't be allowed. I know, with all the soldiers coming back from Iraq, with this very same injury, there is going to be a next time here. What can we do?"

"Nothing, really. He's the judge and he can pretty much say what he wants, even if it is out of line," Frank said.

We left the courtroom with poor Dave still asking what had been said, me fuming and Libby telling me that "Really, it was OK Mom, he was nice to me." That poor child just didn't understand what had happened. Thank God.

On the drive home, several times, Libby questioned me about being better. She really believed that because the judge had told her so, then her headaches, fatigue and memory problems would all just go away. I didn't know what to say, so I just told her that it would be really nice if it happened that way. I fumed inside.

For several days I thought about what had happened in that courtroom and finally I called Frank and asked him if it would hurt Libby's case if I wrote a letter to the judge. He said it shouldn't hurt a thing and thought it was a good idea, however if I really decided to write one, make sure the judge knew it was my own idea. Frank would have to appear in front of him again and didn't want that to interfere with any other case.

I agreed and spent an entire day drafting a letter to the judge.

> *Dear Judge,*
>
> *I'm writing this letter in regards to a conversation that you had with my daughter, Elizabeth, in your courtroom this week, regarding her mild traumatic brain injury. As her mother, I think you should be aware of the implications of your words.*
>
> *Because of her injury, Libby has difficulty understanding some conversations. In school if a teacher gave instructions, she would try to follow them to the letter (if she could remember them), so, on the way home from court, Libby was excited to think that, because someone of high importance told her that her brain would now heal itself, because the lawsuit was over, she isn't going to have any more migraines, fatigue, or memory impairments, all because you said so. How could you say to her that "Now that her lawsuit was*

over, she didn't have to have symptoms anymore and that she could now recover?" Or "That, because you had an accident two years ago and were injured, but quickly recovered, because you didn't bring a lawsuit and therefore didn't "Have to" have symptoms. I'm glad she didn't understand the implications of those statements, it would have crushed her.

Naturally, she wants to be fully recovered and as her parents we want the same for her. But the reality of it is she isn't. Her stamina is good for about four days and then she has to take a day to recover enough to be able to function as a normal seventeen year old does. Our vacations no longer last for two weeks because we have to include days of rest. There are no lawyers, or doctors around when she goes to the mall, like normal teenagers do, and there are no lawyers or doctors there the following day, when she has to stay in bed, because she over did it at the mall. As her mother, I tried to keep her life as normal as possible, in hopes that she would fully recover. I didn't include her in a lot of the legal conversations, but took care of as much as I could without involving her, so to imply to her that now that "it's over" her brain can tell her to get better is so preposterous! When I heard you telling Libby that, I was shocked.

One of the hardest things about her recovery has been the lack of understanding or knowledge about this injury. It is NOT just a concussion. I had a concussion, my son has had one and so has my husband. We recovered, some in a couple of weeks and some in a couple of months, but we all recovered, and we never once sued anyone. When after three months, Libby still didn't remember that she'd taken Algebra and Spanish the year before and still didn't recognize people from her past, we knew it was more than just a concussion. For the past three years the Brain Injury Assoc. and I have presented a class at

Libby's school for any teachers interested in learning about TBI. Her teachers always start out supportive and understanding, but when faced with the reality of what Libby goes through, by Christmas, we are at the school again fighting for her rights and trying to help teachers understand, that just because they've lost patience, it doesn't make this injury go away.

I have studied TBI extensively, looking for answers why my daughter could still have deficits and it not show up on all the conventional, medical scans and what I found is that 15% of all TBI's never show up. This past year, because of all the soldiers coming home from Iraq with this very same injury, (which is now considered the signature injury of the war) Bethesda Naval Hospital is now using a new scan called a DTI that actually shows that the damage in mild TBI patients tends to be in the white matter surrounding the brain. None of our conventional scans can see the white matter, which is why the injury doesn't show up. So the TBI is also now being attributed to the injury in the matter surrounding the brain and not just the brain itself. Unfortunately, Libby's injury happened almost 3 years ago when this technology wasn't being used yet.

Our goal in this lawsuit was not just about money. It was also about how the school handled the accident. Libby was left on the bus for an hour, even after being seen by a nurse who told her she was fine. No EMT's were called, even though, when I finally got Libby to the ER later that evening, 7 other children were there too from her bus. And in that entire first year, when Libby started coming back to school, NO accommodations were ever given to her, only excuses why the school couldn't treat her any differently than any other student. I learned the part 200 Regulations of the Dept. of Education; had to contact the Advocacy Center and the Brain Injury Assoc. just to get what few accommodations we now have for our daughter. We left the knowledge of the law to our attorney and after all our struggles along the way we learned that we needed that concrete piece of evidence such as a MRI or CT to really prove Libby had a long term injury. We settled, because we took our lawyers advice (and I do think rightfully so especially after hearing your conversation with Libby). We fought so hard with the school district over these past three years just to have some accommodations that if this case were thrown out of court; we could lose everything we'd worked so hard to get. Libby's dream is to be either a music teacher or music therapist. Both require at least 4 years of college. She is determined to go and her dad and I are just as determined to see her fulfill that dream.

The medical world has come a long way in the study of brain injuries, but still has a long way to go and the laws are even further behind the times. I have devoted some of my time since Libby's injury in helping educate people on what a mild TBI really is. I volunteer with the BIANYS and have helped with TBI classes at school. During the county fair our group from BIANYS is helping the Sheriff's Dept. and Kiwanis Club, hand out bike helmets and literature about TBI. I invite you to stop by the booth and learn a little more about this injury and the consequences of what it can do to someone. We've met some wonderful people that are TBI survivors and in doing this it's given Libby a better understanding of her injury and also a compassion for the people that are suffering much worse than she is. Even after this case is over, we will continue to help educate others about TBI. When Libby is off to college, my intentions are to continue educating people and work towards stricter laws about how schools handle bus accidents. I'd like to see it be mandatory that EMT's are automatically called to the scene and any child in question is transported to

*the hospital and not have to wait until they get home.
Two hours could have made the difference between life
and death if Libby had actually had a brain bleed. And
of course I'd like to see the laws change to allow for the
fact that the brain sometimes just doesn't do what our
laws say it has to.*

*In writing this my hope is that you have a better
understanding of MTBI so when the next person comes
through your courtroom with a similar injury, please just
take a minute and think before you tell them what you
told Libby. I'm not knowledgeable about the laws, but
I have learned that the brain is a tricky organ and no
one can put a time table on how long it takes to heal, or
what technology the injury is going to show up on. But
it's real and it's devastating, and affects everyone around
the injured person. Many times we said to ourselves. "It
would have been so much easier if she'd broken her arm.
Set it, cast it, let it heal and then get on with life." Not
so with even a mild TBI. I'll leave you with this thought.
If Libby lost 20% of her vocabulary you might think.
"That's not bad." Now look at this letter and remove
every 5th word and read it again. It should be easy right?
After all you're reading at 80%.*

Sincerely,
Naomi Parker

Before I had a chance to think about what I was doing and
second guess myself, I mailed the letter. I didn't expect to hear
from the judge, but it felt great to say everything I wanted to say.
So many people make innocent comments, never realizing how
they may hurt the person they're talking to. This time I wasn't
sure it was so innocent.

Libby and I did go to the county fair and helped hand
out five hundred bike helmets. It was a long, exhausting, but
very rewarding day. I noticed, though, that Libby was easily
angered the week before, but held her emotions in check the

day of the helmet give away. The following few days were horrible for both of us and I just couldn't figure out what was going on. Finally, I told Dave I needed to get away for a couple days, because I could feel depression creeping back. My sister Marge was at the lake and there was always an open invitation to join her and her husband. I packed a bag and left, telling Libby she'd be fine and help take care of Daddy. I asked Dave to do the same thing in reverse.

I stayed two days, soaking up the sun, going on wine tours, eating out and just relaxing. I came home ready to take on the world again. I noticed right away that Libby's mood seemed to have improved while I was gone too.

Several more days went by and I began to notice that Libby's energy level had improved. I finally asked her what was going on. "Mom after that judge talked to me, I decided he was right. I really want to be better. I don't want 504 Plans following me into college. So a couple weeks ago I quit taking all my medicine. Mom I think I feel better without it. I can get up in the morning and get things done."

I didn't know what to say. Libby and I had tried several times before to wean her off her meds. I hated putting all those chemicals into her body. I hated that they made her gain weight, but they served a purpose. They kept her from having anxiety attacks and emotional storms and migraines. Now she wasn't taking anything. At first my anger at the judge welled up again, but I decided before I'd react to what Libby had just told me, I'd watch and wait. Maybe this time she really could get off all her meds. She seemed to be under control; she had been really ugly last week, but that was probably withdrawal from just stopping all her meds at once.

On Friday Libby ran up from the mailbox waving a letter in her hand. "Mom come quick, you have a letter from the judge!" Libby called to me. Excitedly she leaned over my shoulder as I sat down and tore the envelope open. I really hadn't expected a response, but here it was. I hoped it wasn't something awful, or him telling us he'd changed his mind. I began to read.

Dear Ms. Parker,

Thank you for your letter concerning the court appearance at which I approved the settlement of Elizabeth's lawsuit.

Before responding to your comments, I would first like to say that you are to be admired for your dedication to educating people on what a TBI really is, for fighting for positive changes at the school, and in supporting your daughter's dreams for the future. In my position, I encounter a number of uninvolved or absent parents and I see the devastation that causes in the lives of children. I realize nothing you do is for your own recognition, but, for whatever it may be worth, I commend you.

I accept your criticism of my comments to Elizabeth, and I apologize for any distress they have caused you.

We have a family friend who suffered a TBI in a motor vehicle accident. We visited him and his family in the hospital and have seen him many times since his release. His recovery has been slow and steady, but by no means complete. My heart goes out to individuals and families who deal with these issues every day.

Years ago, I was made aware of research which concluded that some litigants' recoveries were improved by the conclusion of their lawsuits, as it was indicated that, despite one's sincere desire to recover from injuries sustained, there appeared to be some uncontrollable subconscious restriction on achieving maximum recovery, almost as if it wouldn't be fair or right to recover while the lawsuit is pending. My purpose was only to refer to this principle as an encouragement.

You wrote that I stated, "now that her lawsuit was over she didn't have to have symptoms any more and that she could now recover." I have reviewed the transcript and my comments were more directed at the rate of recovery than the fact of recovery, i.e. her ability to recover at all. I said,

"Just when you leave here, when you walk out the door here today, you should be able to recover faster and more completely now (that) this case is over than you have been up until today."

It is said that the road to hell is paved with good intentions. It was certainly not my intention to offer false hope, but only to present encouragement for her future progress. In any event, I will have the benefit of your comments for any similar situation in the future.

Sincerely,

I never expected an apology. It was such a wonderful feeling, reading this letter. Never did I imagine that I, a Mom, a nobody, would ever have the brass to not only write a judge, but have him apologize. Three years ago I never would have, but would have meekly accepted whatever he'd said in the court room and probably stewed about it for years. Maybe justice is served once again. Libby gets money for college; the school can't pull anything because they've now admitted liability and we can be done with lawyers, courtrooms and start moving on. As a bonus, because of this mans words, my daughter just may be able to stay off her meds. Maybe some day I'll write him again, thanking him. Now what do I do with all the stuff I've collected just in case we needed it for trial? Hmmmm, maybe have a bonfire and invite a few friends over.

CHAPTER 19

Moving On

Libby is a senior! This is her last year of high school, and yes I can finally say; it really will be her last year. She has passed enough courses and enough Regents exams that she is going to graduate with a Regents diploma. All her courses this year seem fairly easy; no more exhausting state final exams. She's taking Applied Math in place of Algebra that she failed last year. She comes home giggling because it's so easy.

"Today we learned how to use a ruler." She say's. "Really, Mom it's that easy."

We went last week and had Libby's new neuropsych exams that we had scheduled earlier this summer, back when we needed them for court. I decided that I wanted to know just how much Libby had improved over these past three years medically. Did we need her 504 Plan to follow her into college? I wasn't sure. So we kept our scheduled appointment with Dr. Rogers and Libby went for her testing. It was a grueling eight full hours. Libby climbed into the car exhausted.

"I hope I never have to do that again. I hated it." She said, from the passenger seat, as she lowered the seat back into a reclining position. She refused to talk much about it on the way home, so I really had no idea what had happened or what type of testing Dr. Rogers had actually performed. Libby was sure, though, she'd done horrible. "Everything was hard, a lot harder than the last time," was all she would say.

My heart sank, I secretly was hoping that Libby would fly through this series of testing and Dr. Rogers would tell us she was all better. I knew that wasn't likely to happen, but since Libby had stopped taking her meds, I noticed a huge improvement in her stamina. She seemed a little more scattered in her thoughts, but my old cheerful Libby who got up and did what she needed to do was making her presence known again. She'd had the summer to relax, sleep, bring her energy level back up, plan for her senior year, and to let her body adjust to the lack of medications she'd been taking for almost three years.

We visited her first choice in colleges and spent the day there as Libby was led around the Music Education Building. She even got to take a lesson from the violin instructor there.

"That's it; this is where I want to be." Libby said dreamily as she looked around the campus. "It feels like home."

Being the typical worry wart that I am, I reminded Libby that she also needed to be accepted by the college before she could go. I received the only dirty look from her that whole day.

We encouraged Libby to check out other colleges, just in case she wasn't accepted there, but she was adamant and refused to look at any others.

"If I don't get in, then I'll look," Libby said. "You guys gotta start having faith in me," she said smiling.

My little girl was growing up right before my eyes. She was looking at her future with high expectations. Nothing was going to stand in her way. The only difference was it was our new Libby, a mix between the pre-accident daughter we had always loved, and the new young woman, who now stood looking at college buildings with high hopes for what she would become.

We went back to Dr. Rogers a few days after his testing, for a general update on the results.

"Well, Libby," Dr. Rogers began. "How do you think you did?"

"I don't know. It was hard, though." Libby responded shaking her head.

"Well, do you think you did better or worse than last time?" He asked, with his professional smile pasted on his face.

"I know it was a lot harder, so I probably did worse." Libby said, tentatively. "But I hope I did better."

"What was the hardest for you?" Dr. Rogers asked, still feeling Libby out, before giving her the results.

"Math, definitely the math. I think I did really bad in that," Libby said, scowling.

Dr. Rogers laughed and said, "Yes, you're right, you did really bad in Math, so now that the worst is out of the way, let's go over the rest."

He spent about an hour going over each of the tests, sometimes going into detail about where Libby had improved and where she hadn't. One of the biggest things, that showed improvement, was in her working memory. He explained that he felt she'd improved in that area because she'd now trained her brain to create a visual, to help her remember. He used two words as an example; "Suitcase and blue". When Libby explained that she made sentences to remember the words, such as "The suitcase is blue," Dr. Rogers asked her if she actually pictured a blue suitcase, in her mind, and she agreed she did. He smiled and explained, that's what visualization was.

In her visual spatial relations, Libby excelled. Anything that had to do with putting things together or picking details out of a picture, Libby scored in the 98th percentile. Libby loved photography. That explained why she was so good at it. In almost all the areas that Libby thought she did horrible in, she actually scored either normal or high normal with the exception of being able to focus and concentrate. She scored in the 16th percentile when asked to focus on information provided to her that was delivered in a flat monotone way. Once voice inflection was added, she improved. That would explain why, at times, she wouldn't "remember" certain information that had been delivered in a data only form. It had actually never even been absorbed by her brain, so how could she be expected to remember?

It also explained why the animated teachers did so much better than the teachers that delivered in a "read the text and answer the question" format. Now we had something a little more concrete that might help her teachers.

Overall, Libby improved enough that Dr. Rogers felt that, by the time she reached college, she wouldn't need accommodations as long as she worked on techniques to help her focus when the information got boring. He was thrilled that Libby was off her meds. He said that we just would probably see a marked difference in her stamina, during the school year. He suggested waiting to see if her migraines also would diminish this year, without having to put her back on any preventative medication. The medications she'd been on actually depressed the brain and caused sluggishness.

It's so difficult to know what the right thing is. The meds helped Libby control her migraines, but slowed her down. So does she handle her headaches as they come or trade off that new feeling of energy for fewer headaches? Libby immediately chose more energy, even if it meant more migraines. Her anxiety medication is gone from her system and other than an occasional "teenage and very normal" outburst; she's handling that well, too.

Is her TBI gone? No it's not, but it has improved dramatically. I'm a firm believer that she will continue to heal as time goes on.

Libby came home from school yesterday, bounded up the drive, threw open the door and called to me. "Mom, you'll never guess what I did today!" She was smiling from ear to ear. "It was so embarrassing."

"I don't know. What did you do?" I asked, waiting for her to spill.

"Well, last year 5th period was English and this year it's Economics. Well anyways, it was 5th period and I walked right past Economics and I saw Mr. Crandall look funny at me, but I didn't know why. Well anyways I walked into English and Mrs. Painter was sitting at her desk eating." Libby took a breath.

"Mom, it was so embarrassing. She looked up at me and asked me what I was doing there during her lunch? Then she smiled and asked me if I was coming to English and I said "Yea". Then she told me that I probably ought to check my schedule, because I wasn't in her English anymore." Libby started laughing.

"I said 'Oh crap' and ran out of her room as fast as I could and back down to Economics.

Mr. Crandall saw me come in and said "Hmmmm, go to the wrong class?" and laughed at me."

I laughed and asked. "So what did you tell him?"

Libby screwed her face up, squinching it into a frown, all the while still smiling. "I said 'Noooooo' and sat down real quick, but he laughed at me anyway', cause he knew."

We laughed together at her mishap and it struck me. Two years ago she'd have been in tears when this happened. Today she laughed. Today she came up the drive like the old Libby and chattered away until she told me everything she wanted to say about the day, even though the chatter was a little bit about what TBI does to someone. Today was fun and lighthearted.

Today, she was telling me a story about her two new teachers, both fresh out of college and by any senior girls' standards "Hot", although one was married, so that instantly made him off limits. Libby was skipping back and forth, between the two teachers in her story, and stumbled over one of the teacher's names

. "Mr. Conlin....Conway....Con....Oh, it doesn't matter. Oh yea, it's Congdon, that's right." She continued on with her story without pausing talking a hundred miles an hour, for another five minutes, telling me how much fun they were and how all the girls were trying to make good impressions. Libby laughed.

"Like it matters, cause' he's a teacher and he's going to pay any attention to them like that," she said with a snort and continued on with her story.

So whether she stumbles over someone's name, or forgets where she's going or where she's supposed to be and even if she's measuring with a ruler, instead of complicated trigonometry, it doesn't matter. We can laugh about it, instead of cry. Libby can smile again. We have more and more of those days now, so it's easier to put the difficult stuff aside.

Our new Superintendent has implemented new rules for concussion in our school. All participants of sports have to have a base line physical. If they suffer a concussion, or any other injury, they can't return to the field until they are back to the baseline again. I talked with him this morning. He let me know how interested he was in having Sharon come to the school for more than just a forty minute workshop for Libby's teachers, but to utilize her talents, in other ways, throughout the school too. I knew I liked that man the day I met him.

Libby's TBI still rears its head from time to time. I realized something, today, that I really hadn't thought too much about. I'd been so busy muddling through, doing my best, trying to make life easier for Libby that I forgot to stop and smell the roses. My daughter had turned into an astonishing, funny, fantastic person. Somehow it slipped by me. Whether it's the old Libby, the new one or that wonderful mixture of both, I know with certainty that I love my daughter to the deepest core of my being. Nothing will ever change that.

We had a photographer come to the house, a couple weeks ago, to take Libby's senior picture and she took hundreds. She took some formal, informal, pictures of Libby with our stallion and a barn kitten, down by the pond and in our neighbor's luscious flower garden. Every picture has a real smile. In every picture you can see Libby's personality, just bubbling off the paper. She's truly ready for her senior year.

Libby gave her mare to a friend of ours, who has a daughter just the right age to enjoy horses. Mable now lives three miles down the road and has a new girl's undivided attention. Libby can visit her whenever she wishes, but so far, hasn't asked. Just another of those choices she's had to make in her new normal. The choice was easier for Libby than I thought it would be. She hasn't seemed too down not to see her mare in the pasture. Me

I'm still clinging to my horse, but I, too, think that finding him a good home is probably best.

Watching her go off to college will be bittersweet, just like all the other parents that send their child off into the unknown. I'm sure there will be tears, when that day comes, but for me, the tears will be joyful, because it will be the culmination of all of our efforts to see our daughters' dream come true. The look on Libby's face this summer as she stared at the campus buildings, told me she's ready.

Ready to dream of the future and stop worrying about the past. Ready to face what ever challenges she'll meet this year and beyond. Whether she decides to tell the new people in her life about her experience with TBI, will be her decision because even though she's given her whole hearted permission to write this story, as long as I change the names, she can continue to be just another face in the crowd if she wants to.

Me? I want to shout to the world about my brave, courageous, funny, beautiful daughter. She is my sunshine. I am so proud to know her today. I know something else with certainty; Dave and I will have done our job as parents, to the very best of our ability and I will never have to look back and wish I'd done this or taken that action, and Libby will be ready for whatever comes next. *Just wait and see.*

The End

ACKNOWLEDGEMENTS

There are many people I wish to thank for all their support throughout our TBI journey. Without them, Libby's story could have had a very different ending. To all Libby's teachers who took the initiative and helped her without those written accommodations, I thank you. There are good teachers and good schools out there.

To Kelly Cornish, our first angel, you have a deep understanding of what is needed for students with disabilities. I hope you never give up helping them. You made such a difference in Libby's life. You were so brave to speak on Libby's behalf. We will never forget you.

Sharon Johnson, where do I begin? You've been there for us every step of the way, willing to do whatever it took. Your job with BIANYS should earn you your angel wings, because you do so much more than just a job. You help so many people, but still managed to make time, every time we needed you.

Sharon Marella from Parent to Parent, the service you provide is so valuable to parents with children who have disabilities. Thank you so much for taking time out of your busy schedule to include Libby and our family.

Jean Tydings, again, thank you just doesn't seem to say enough. Without your services from The Advocacy Center, I never would have known how to "fight right". You were the first one to tell me that it was OK to feel angry. Then you taught me how to take my anger and turn it into a positive.

For any readers, I have included information on the three organizations that assisted us in our journey and kept the names of the people that helped us. Sharon Johnson, Sharon Marella and Jean Tydings and the three organizations BIANYS, Parent to Parent and The Advocacy Center are very real and are out there to help those parents who struggle with getting their child's needs met educationally, physically, medically and socially.

My hope, in writing our story, is that if there are any readers out there struggling with some of the same issues we did, you take the time to find these places that helped us. The search isn't easy, but the benefits are so worth the effort. The information and support, from these three places, were invaluable to Libby's success. I can never repay all the kindness and generosity. I am deeply grateful to all of you.

Most of all, I want to thank my family. Dave, you put up with all of it and were that steady rock both Libby and I needed. Libby, you truly are my sunshine. Your smile brightens my world. I know that, what you went through no one should have to, but you are a real survivor. Thank you for letting me tell our story.

The Advocacy Center
590 South Avenue
Rochester, NY 14620
585-546-1700
www.advocacycenter.com

The Advocacy Center builds the capacity of individuals with disabilities and their families to advocate for themselves, realize their personal goals, and make positive changes in their lives and in their communities.

Through information-sharing, educational workshops, individual advocacy support, and independent service coordination, we advance people's knowledge and skills and improve their access to resources and services. Our leadership development programs prepare individuals to help others as volunteer lay advocates and agents for positive change in their communities.

We offer workshops and conferences for professionals to enhance their effectiveness interacting with or supporting individuals with disabilities and their families. Hands-on disability awareness workshops are available for any community group.

The Advocacy Center is a Parent Training and Information Center funded by the United States Department of Education and a Special Education Parent Center funded by the New York State Education Department.

Brain Injury Association of New York State

10 Colvin Avenue
Albany, NY 12206-1242

Telephone (518) 459-7911 • Fax (518) 482-5285
Family Help Line (800) 228-8201
Website: www.bianys.org • E-mail: info@bianys.org

FACTS Services is a free service provided by BIANYS

1. Family Advocacy
2. Educational Advocacy
3. Outreach
4. Prevention
5. Training

FACTS Service Definitions

1. **Family Advocacy:** support and counseling surrounding family issues following brain injury, connecting family with funding resources, housing, transportation and service providers.
2. **Educational Advocacy:** support and counseling surrounding educational needs after brain injury, helping family with the IEP process, attendance at CSE meetings.
3. **Outreach:** connection with service providers, hospitals, schools, human service agencies, community-based and governmental agencies to increase awareness of BIANYS, ABI/TBI and increasing FACTS program enrollment.
4. **Prevention:** Connection with service providers, hospitals, schools, human service agencies, community-based and governmental agencies to teach injury prevention and safety.
5. **Training:** Connection with service providers, hospitals, schools, human service agencies, community-based and governmental agencies to conduct trainings about TBI/ABI.

FACTS Eligibility

- Documentation of ABI/TBI before 22 years of age
- If no documentation exists, a doctor or specialist must make determination based upon neuropsychological test data
- Permanent NYS address

Contact:

Sharon Johnson
BIANYS FACTS Coordinator
315-538-8018
sjohnson@bianys.org
www.bianys.org BIANYS family helpline: 1-800-228-8201

Parent to Parent of NYS

Parent to Parent of NYS is a statewide not for profit organization with a mission to support and connect families of individuals with special needs. We are a point of contact for many parents who are 'getting started' on their journey of parenting a child with developmental disabilities. There are 14 offices throughout NYS, staffed by Regional Coordinators, who are parents or close relatives of individuals with special needs. A website is maintained to provide information and events listings - www.parenttoparentnys.org

A Support Parent Network of over 1200 parents is the backbone of the **Parent Matching Program.** It has been created and is maintained by Parent to Parent Regional Coordinators. This is a model program used across the country to put parents in touch on a one to one basis with other parents who have a child with a chronic illness or disability. "Support Parents" are parents of individuals with special needs who have made the offer to speak one to one with "new" parents and share their experiences. Support parents are the key to this program. The organization recognizes the need for emotional support as well as the importance of parents knowing they are not alone.

When parents agree to be Support Parents, they are provided a skills building training, which includes an overview of how the program works, an understanding of the stages and emotions a parent or caregiver may be experiencing, as well as listening skills. New parents are welcome to join the Support Parent network and to share their experience.

In addition to the Parent Matching program, the organization fields telephone calls from parents of children with special needs who are looking for resources, services and information. Calls include parents looking for information about medical services and therapies and those looking for information specifically about an illness or disability. There are often questions about special education. All programs are based on the philosophy of parents helping each other, drawing on a network of parents helping parents. Coordinators are there to assist, but draw on other parents to help. There is no charge for services.

The Family to Family Health Care Information Center assists families with access to health care, health care recordkeeping and transition from pediatric to adult health care. Information about this program can be viewed at the website. http://www.parenttoparentnys.org/Family2Family/familytofamily.html

CPSIA information can be obtained
at www.ICGtesting.com
Printed in the USA
LVHW02s2329251217
560740LV00001B/68/P